THE
McPherson
PRINCIPLE

THE
McPherson
PRINCIPLE

An Innovative Approach
to Hitting the Bullseye of
Revenue Cycle Performance

MICHAEL L. DUKE

White River Press
Amherst, Massachusetts

First published 2021 by White River Press
Amherst, Massachusetts 01004 • whiteriverpress.com

Book and cover design by Lufkin Graphic Designs
Norwich, Vermont 05055 • www.LufkinGraphics.com

ISBN: 978-1-887043-99-1 (paperback)
       978-1-935052-75-3 (ebook)

Library of Congress Cataloging-in-Publication Data

Names: Duke, Michael L., 1969- author.
Title: The McPherson principle : an innovative approach to hitting the
   bullseye of revenue cycle performance / Michael L. Duke.
Description: Amherst, Massachusetts : White River Press, [2021] | Summary:
   "Through reading this book, the reader will discover new approaches and
   concepts related to business rule-driven work tasking and automation,
   augmented analytics explicitly designed to solve root cause issues
   within revenue cycle operations, natural language"-- Provided by
   publisher.
Identifiers: LCCN 2021021045 | ISBN 9781887043991 (paperback)
Subjects: LCSH: Business--Fiction. | Revenue management--Fiction. | LCGFT:
   Novels.
Classification: LCC PS3604.U4327 M37 2020 | DDC 813/.6--dc23
LC record available at https://lccn.loc.gov/2021021045

DEDICATION

I WOULD LIKE TO DEDICATE THIS BOOK to two influential personalities in my life who sadly are no longer with us. First, the lead character is named after one of my lifelong friends, Bill Mitsch. Bill and I knew each other through a few bad times and several great ones. He helped shape my view of life. From a professional perspective, Bill's explanation to me of how he used analytics and sensors to monitor skyscraper elevator maintenance protocols, gave me the idea on how to identify revenue cycle failure points through data and how to monitor these points to understand breakdowns and identify processes before they would fail. I will always be indebted to him for his friendship and guidance. I miss Bill every day.

Second, I would be remiss if I did not also dedicate this work to Wayne McPherson. Wayne was a partner at Deloitte Consulting when he took a chance on a young and unpolished kid coming into the industry, one who could barely spell Revenue Cycle, let alone understand it. Through more patience than most firm partners would have provided, and his keen interest in my personal wellbeing, I learned how to effectively manage and improve revenue cycle operations; more importantly, he provided a model of how to be a true professional and consultant. I honestly would not be where I am today without his guidance and belief that I could be successful. I think of Wayne constantly and work very hard to live up to the high standards he impressed upon me. I'm honored to be able to use his surname in the title.

ACKNOWLEDGMENTS

I WOULD LIKE to use this space to acknowledge two individuals who made this book possible. First, my wonderful wife, Rebecca. She believes that I can do anything I put my mind to and pushes me like no other. It was this belief that enabled me to drive forward once I had figured out that this would be a yearlong endeavor.

Second, I would be remiss if I did not acknowledge one individual from our marketing team at Baker Tilly, John Steger. When I brought to his attention that I would like to write this book he never hesitated, was highly supportive, and assisted in navigating the early stages of getting started. It was his lack of hesitation that allowed me to jump in without worrying about whether I could really pull it off.

CONTENTS

FOREWORD

THROUGH ALMOST THIRTY YEARS working as a management consultant in healthcare, I've had the distinct pleasure of meeting and working with countless smart, creative, solution-oriented professionals striving to make the U.S. healthcare system work better—and if I am completely honest, a handful just trying to make a buck off the chaos and inefficiency. Mike Duke is the epitome of the former. Because attaining and maintaining peak revenue cycle performance has proven to be one of the most vexing and intractable challenges for the industry, I am often asked by healthcare leaders, executive recruiters, and aspiring consultants about it. My go-to answer for years has been, "Let me connect you with the most innovative thinker and committed practitioner I know in that space: Mike Duke." Or if it was my client asking, I called Duke for advice.

In 1997, Wayne McPherson, a partner at Deloitte Consulting who led one of the nation's premier revenue cycle consultancies at the time, had what must have seemed, on paper, to the Deloitte recruiting team as the inauspicious idea to hire Duke and myself "onto his island of misfit toys." Neither of us (nor anyone else in Wayne's practice) had a national MBA school pedigree, just a few years of related industry experience and apparently some *je ne sais quoi* that he could discern. With a collective Deloitte experience of fifteen days, Duke, one other newbie, and I were deployed on our first engagement. In the weeks that followed, we committed innumerable rookie mistakes, pulled repeated all-nighters, and produced a gruesome first draft of the assessment report, but in the end, we found tens of millions in opportunity for the client and hatched a lasting, trusted friendship along with an "off-the-books skunk works" (my slang for a lot of late night work that wasn't sanctioned but was highly effective) for solving client problems that still endures. From that first project to this day, what I always see in Duke is an insatiable curiosity, a relentless drive to get it right rather than to be right, and an unquenchable passion to help healthcare provider organizations flourish.

Many of the nascent (at least in healthcare) technological innovations of the current moment—such as robotic process automation, artificial intelligence, natural language processing, and augmented analytics—create a massive opportunity for the revenue cycle industry to reimagine the way work gets done, dramatically elevate effectiveness and productivity, and create prolonged financial improvement. One of the greatest historical challenges in revenue cycle has been sustainability; even the best improvement efforts of the past have required exceptional effort, focus, and manual intervention to prevent slippage. These emerging technologies provide a practical path to elevated, long-term performance.

I have worked with Duke and observed in him this kind of innovative thinking and application of technology since our early days at Deloitte. Whether scouring through SMS INVISION user manuals in search of optimal workflows, building a custom Access database to enable the HIM practice to help defend providers in OIG audits, identifying novel methods of data extraction that unlocked vast troves of previously inaccessible information, championing the power of data visualization to inform management decisions, or myriad other examples, Duke carries on a ceaseless quest to deliver fresh vision for the revenue cycle by melding deep yet inventive operational knowledge with technological possibility.

In the spirit of Eliyahu M. Goldratt's *The Goal*[1], this book takes us on the fictionalized but very real journey of a team of revenue cycle professionals rising to meet the challenges and opportunities of this moment in the U.S. healthcare system. The team must confront entrenched interests and outdated modes of work, thread the needle of competing demands and stakeholders, and traverse murky organizational politics—the everyday tangle of every revenue cycle professional's life—to find success with unconventional operational and technological solutions. The novel elucidates a rich perspective and pioneering course to transform revenue cycle operations and translates them into an entertaining, relatable, and achievable example of how healthcare financial professionals can rise to meet this seminal moment.

I hope you find it as enjoyable and astute as I do, and that you discover at least some nuggets, if not a full lode, of applicable and executable insights that will help you thrive as you do the often unsung but invaluable yeoman's work of keeping our health systems financially sound—or better yet, excelling.

—Doug Long
Partner & Healthcare Practice Leader
McMann & Ransford

---

1 Goldratt, Eliyahu M., *The Goal: A Process of Ingoing Improvement,* 3rd ed. (Great Barrington, MA: North River Press, 2012).

INTRODUCTION

*T*HE *MCPHERSON PRINCIPLE* is about new ways to understand operational performance related to the Revenue Cycle ecosystem in the healthcare industry and is named after one of the smartest individuals I have ever known, Wayne McPherson. This new understanding is intended to improve management insight and move the needle on making performance enhancements that fundamentally change the financial outcomes of a healthcare organization.

This book is a work of fiction that illustrates how people trying to solve their business issues have to think in unconventional ways to allow them to develop a deeper understanding of business operations. The issue most of the time is that people see problems from their historical perspective, and most of them are willing to tell you "why" something cannot be accomplished rather than open their mind to new concepts and ideas. This is normal human behavior, but if we are serious about improving, then the pursuit of new ideas must be incorporated into our daily lives.

There are two primary reasons that I wrote this novel. First, I wanted to make the concepts of revenue cycle performance improvement more relatable and, quite honestly, easier to digest than your typical business book. By placing them in a fictional environment similar to those individuals currently grinding away in the industry, I hope that the relationship with the core components of the McPherson Principle will make sense. Secondly, I also wanted to convey that just because we do something one way, it doesn't make it the best way. If I can show an organization how to achieve higher financial outcomes, and it takes a different approach that serves the organization's mission of great healthcare for the local community, then that is what I want to do.

I wrote this novel in the spirit of Eli Goldratt, who authored many interesting books but especially *The Goal*, and I highly recommend you read it. That novel set me on a path of operational performance improvement that I hope to never leave.

I wish you luck on the journey that is continuous improvement for Revenue Cycle operations. If our paths cross, I welcome the opportunity to discuss the McPherson Principle with you.

BILL MATTHEWS

March 8

Beep! . . . Beep! . . . Beep!

THE OBNOXIOUS SOUND of the alarm at 6:00 a.m. roused me from my deep slumber. But it was the other sound of my vibrating phone that really got my attention; I stretched out my hand to grab it from the bedside table. The only light in the pitch-black bedroom, the screen showed five notifications—three work emails and two texts from Dave, a member of my management team at Jackson Health System (JHS).

"What time is it?" The groggy voice of my wife, Susan, came from behind me as she raised her head slightly from the pillow.

"Just a little after six, hon. Go back to sleep. No reason for you to wake up yet."

"Oh, okay. Turn off the alarm, please." The woman I had been married to for ten blissful years burrowed deeper under the covers. As I paused to look at her lying beside me, I had to smile at her tousled hair. I had been lucky in regard to my personal life. Not every day was easy, but being married to your best friend made life a lot of fun.

These thoughts were interrupted by the irritating vibration of the mobile I was still holding. Apparently, Dave couldn't wait any longer to convey the details of whatever issue he felt important enough to bother me with at six o'clock in the morning. I quietly stood up from the bed so as not to disturb Susan more than I already had, and I moved to a chair in the living room. My position at work as VP of Revenue Cycle Management came with some perks—a house in a good neighborhood, a nice car, and yearly educational trips paid for by the hospital.

The benefits partially made up for the fact that I could not spend as much time with my family as most people desire. Work took up a lot of my time, and on occasion I had to stay late or bring work home. Susan understood that I worked hard so I could take better care of our family, but sometimes I wished I had a normal nine-to-five desk job. The stress that came from holding a demanding position was starting to take a toll on my overall health and relationships.

"What is it, Dave?" Without intention, my voice sounded irritated even to my ears as I rang him back.

"Boss, I might be a bit late to the meeting today. Have to take our dog to the vet."

"You kept texting me at six a.m. to tell me this?"

"I wasn't sure how early you'd be in today, and I didn't want to miss you."

"All right. Just send me whatever you have prepared. Overall revenue cycle performance is at an all-time low, and we need to fix it soon."

"Will do. I have some ideas for improving the performance. I'll share them once I get there."

"Sure. Is there anything else you want to talk about?"

"No. Sorry if I woke you."

"You didn't. See you later, Dave."

I stood up and walked to the kitchen to make coffee and some toast. This was my usual daily morning routine; I learned it from my great aunt Minnie who lived to 107, so I figured she must have been doing something right. Getting up early let my mind ponder various subjects without distractions. On top of that, Susan likes coffee first thing in the morning, so I scored bonus points on most days by making it before she got out of bed.

I looked out the window while the machine brewed. The trees were coming alive with green from the spring showers that seemed to be coming every other day. This was my favorite time of year. It used to be fall, I would joke, because you could smell football season, but over the past few years it had switched to the opposite time of year when the air was still cool enough to be refreshing but had lost the severity of winter. The rebirth of everything reminded me that there was always a chance to enjoy another day in the dance of life.

As my gaze moved back from the window to the coffee, I started to think about the coming day and began to wander in my mind through the life that sometimes seemed like a maze. On some mornings, I reflected on how far I had come, about my wife and three beautiful kids, and about life in general. Lately, however, I'd been thinking of only one thing—work. It's strange how something that used to give me joy now seemed like such a frustration. Work had always been a challenge, a fervent endeavor, but now was reduced to a constant pain in my ass.

As one of the largest tertiary health systems in South Carolina, JHS served a diverse patient base from all over the state. It was one of the best facilities in the region and had plans for expansion. Unfortunately, overall financial performance had remained stagnant for months. In fact, it had been going down recently, which was a cause for immense concern and the reason for the meeting scheduled for later today.

Sadly enough, it was during my tenure that the revenue cycle performance had begun to decline, even though the patient population had stayed relatively constant. In addition, thanks to the lackluster performance, accounts receivable had increased due to an uptick in insurance payment denials, which were creating a backlog and increasing revenue leakage. This, of course, had caused a slow but steady decline in cash flow. Perhaps this was not a factor, but the only real market change had been the closure of some local textile plants, although other businesses had arrived to help offset that initial drop in employed individuals with good-paying insurance. Even more of a concern, most of that economic change was only recent, and not at all reflective of the slow and steady decline that had engulfed JHS.

I paused that train of thought and briefly contemplated my career choice. Essentially, revenue cycle management is the people, processes, and technology used by healthcare systems to drive reimbursement, primarily through insurance companies, from a patient's initial appointment to the payment of their final balance. Within the revenue cycle are three major functions: Patient Access, or all the intake activities to clear a patient prior to admission; Revenue Assurance, or the areas that manage charges and apply billing codes for service; and Patient Financial Services, which handles the physical part of getting claims out the door and following up on unpaid ones.

I kept thinking: *I've looked at everything, and I've asked my management team to review it all as well. What are we missing? Sure, we don't always see eye-to-eye with some of the solutions presented, but the group really does want to help and make a difference. Doesn't it?*

The gurgling of the coffee maker captured my attention. Walking to the cupboard, I removed the sugar and dry milk while idly humming a country song that I'd sung the previous night to Mack, our four-year-old, before tucking him into bed. As usual, he didn't want to sleep, judging from the many times he asked for an encore performance. Abbie, his younger sister, was less rambunctious and calmer, yin and yang personified. And then there was the eldest, Amanda, the little mother hen always looking after her siblings.

Stirring the coffee, I thought back to the early days of my marriage to Susan. More than once she told me it had been my adventurous and fun-loving nature that attracted her to a younger me; name it and I would have done it. We even went backpacking across Europe for our honeymoon! But over the years, my increasing role at work meant I had to leave my adventuring days behind and resign myself to a routine and stable life. Yes, it was a great life because of my family, but sometimes I wished I could still run away when the pressure at work mounted to inconceivable levels. Like I could disappear to the beach or the mountains and escape the daily hustle.

Members of the management team had started to blame each other for JHS's increasingly poor performance, as well as the people above them for not providing the right tools to help manage their teams better. Dave had requested additional full-time employees in order to keep up with the mounting backlogs, although so far, I had been pushing back on that idea, because it just didn't seem like the right approach. But other than the minor skirmishes the team members had with each other, they really did get along well and wanted to make a difference; that was the main reason I had any belief at all that we could turn things around.

At the moment, however, I had more important things to think about, namely getting the kids ready for preschool and giving momma bear her elixir of life. Holding the steaming beverage in my hand, I entered the bedroom.

"Wake up," I said gently. "Your coffee is ready."

"Argh, what time is it? That smells divine. Thank you."

"You're welcome. It's almost six-forty. Do you want anything to eat?"

"No, I'll grab something later."

This was a typical morning in the Matthewses' household. The two of us split duties; I was responsible for making breakfast and getting the kids ready for school, while Susan dropped them off and picked them up, as well as made lunches.

I hoped that the meeting today would prove to be just as productive.

At exactly 7:30 a.m., after a hug from each kid, I was in my car. JHS was fifteen minutes away, and the drive featured beautiful countryside, yet the thoughts swirling in my mind were anything but comforting. The past couple of months had been really difficult, and this meeting could very well decide what the financial future of the entire organization would look like.

Ron Baldwin, the CEO of JHS, had been there for over twenty years, shepherding the facility's growth from a single hospital into a complex healthcare system. He'd always had a paternal attitude toward employees and generally did not enforce individual accountability, often stating, "I've seen them grow, and they are good people." I, however, lived in a world where individual performance profoundly mattered, and therefore, the first concern was understanding the issues and finding a solution that worked for everyone. If need be, that meant finding different solutions specially tailored for a variety of individuals' job functions.

Innovation? I wondered. *What can we possibly innovate in the world of revenue cycle?* I decided with a smile that I might be half mad. Only half mad, mind you, because I hadn't answered while talking to myself.

With that thought in mind, I arrived at my destination. The glass windows of the hospital, sparkling brightly against the morning sun, greeted me as I moved briskly towards the entrance, which bustled with people hurrying inside and out. My office was on the second floor, and even though there was an elevator in the building, I took the stairs as I always did. As I passed through the open floor plan, my office door came in view. The polished plaque embossed with my name and position did not bring the same sense of pleasure it used to, but it still conveyed the fact that I took my responsibilities seriously.

Fast forward my day to one of the early management meetings that seem to occur constantly. It went by in a blur as my mind was elsewhere.

"Bill, do you have a moment?" Ron, our stalwart CEO, asked as the rest of my team staggered out of the meeting.

"Sure, Ron, what is it?" I stuck my head out the door to let my administrative assistant, Shannon, know that I might be late for my next meeting. It promised to be a long day.

"I'm not announcing the news publicly just yet, but I wanted you to be one of the first people to know. I've decided to resign."

"*WHAT?*" I spun around so fast I dropped my phone.

"I've developed some health issues that won't let me spend as much time on JHS as I should. It's time for me to step down."

The news about Ron's declining health was not news at all. He had been admitted into the hospital twice in the last three months. It made sense, as he was not a young man anymore, but it was still difficult to picture JHS without him.

"Ron, who can possibly fill your shoes?"

"Well, the Board has conducted a confidential search and has recently hired someone. They'll hopefully introduce him soon, but that individual will most likely have their own management style. As for you, don't worry, just keep on doing what you think is best. I have faith in you and your abilities."

Stunned, I didn't know what to say. We awkwardly shook hands and left the room, both going in separate directions.

Would the new CEO be as easy to work with?

THE NEW CEO

March 27

SITTING AT MY DESK, I looked over the previous month's operational performance review that had been presented to the revenue cycle committee. God, how I've always hated that meeting. It seems like every manager in the organization attends and nothing ever gets accomplished. At some point, management by consensus grew roots at JHS, and we've never been able to shake it. When everyone has an equal part of the decision-making process, sometimes it feels like the only thing that gets accomplished is a lot of talking.

As I looked at the date on the reports, it hit me that it already had been two weeks since Ron's successful retirement party. It was painfully clear how much impact Ron had made on the entire health system and with the staff in general. He was naturally a people-person and cared about the employees themselves, not just their performance at work. Thinking about the party led me to consider the new CEO, Terry Scarborough, whom I was to meet shortly. Not the man himself, but specifically concerns about how he would compare to Ron.

I have to be on my game for this meeting, I thought. *I wish I had more time to prepare solid materials.*

I felt some trepidation when it came to the introductory meeting. Other than that he was taking over Ron's CEO role, I knew little about the man, and I had no idea how his personality would fit with the organization.

My thoughts came to a halt when four of the most important people in my management team stepped in: Kim Sanders, my executive director and right hand; Dave Daniels, my favorite early morning texting team member as well as patient financial services director; Kyle Martin, the patient access director; and Michelle Green, my director of health information management. I waved for them to sit, and they jumped right in.

"So, have we learned anything about Terry yet?" Kim asked.

"I heard from the office grapevine that he's a tough nut," Kyle responded. "Aggressive. Not really the touchy-feely type."

"I've heard this too," I managed to say, hopefully without revealing much frustration at the incessant rumor mill. "But he has a lot of experience in the industry, and hopefully he'll be just what the hospital needs, especially right now. Have any of you thought to run last quarter's performance reports?"

"I was told the meeting was just going to be introductory," said Dave.

"Me, too, but you never know," I responded. "It's fine, I'll do it myself. Any questions you want to make sure I cover?"

"I think it would be important if you can figure out what kind of support we can expect for our current initiatives." Kim was always practical.

"Of course, Kim. That's at the top of my list."

This elicited a chuckle from Dave. "Boss, as you always tell us, 'Go stupid early.' If we don't have a full answer, we are definitely not going to fake it.'" He was right. I had trained them that we were in the business of "knowing" things and not guessing, so if you didn't really know the answer it was better to stop talking.

"Are you suggesting that I tell the new CEO I don't know the answers to his questions? I'm sure that'll go over great." Sarcasm dripped from my statement.

"My coders need help getting through their backlog," Michelle said. "We can't even trust the basic productivity numbers we're getting. Can you add that to the list?"

And so our conversation continued, useful yet casual. Although our management team was small in number, we more than made up for it in dedication and loyalty to each other and JHS. Yes, we disagreed at times, but the hunger to learn from each other gelled us tightly together. The reason behind this team chemistry was deliberate: I was committed to open communication even if it caused an argument. I had played sports my entire life and had witnessed firsthand how a team could accomplish things once thought impossible, as long as everyone communicated openly and were all focused on the same goal.

As is the case in every workplace, rampant office politics tried to pry the tightknit group apart on more than one occasion. However, this management team—nay, this group of friends— stood by each other, as well as for the betterment of the health system through thick and thin, and I would not accept anything else. Yes, the performance of the organization was currently a bit worse than in previous years, but I was satisfied and proud of all four of them and was sure we could successfully tackle this problem and get out of our current slump.

Surely the new CEO will bring some new ideas? Maybe this wasn't such a bad thing? Then again, it's better to keep expectations low and see what happens.

It was late afternoon, time for me to meet our new CEO, and I was running behind schedule. A few minutes ago I'd been informed that the meeting would not be held in the conference room but in Rebecca Davis's office.

Rebecca was the CFO of the health system and a great person to work for. Her understanding nature and excellent problem-solving skills had converted skeptics into admirers over the years, as well as into loyal and committed employees. JHS was in safe financial hands under her watch. Although she spent more time on the general financial aspects of the hospital and relied heavily on my expertise as far as revenue cycle performance was concerned, she was the type of boss who was happy regardless of the operational decisions made, as long as expected performance levels were achieved by the overall system.

I quickly crossed the main area of the second floor, bounded down the stairs (two at a time), and entered the administration corridor that held Rebecca's office as well as Terry's. I was out of breath once I arrived, so I took a few seconds to compose myself and wipe the sweat from my brow before knocking and entering. I was assuming simplicity in the meeting—it would be just the three of us, with Rebecca introducing me to the new CEO, followed by a small chat regarding my role—and I figured it should only take about a half hour, as I was sure Rebecca had already given Terry an overview of my department's performance.

The room was a little tidier than normal, but, as usual, the space was highlighted by Rebecca's restaurant-quality espresso machine. As the CFO, she was entitled to some perks, and she definitely loved her specialty coffees.

Rebecca was seated behind her desk, her hands on top of two folders. Even though she was in her fifties, she looked decades younger, no doubt from her daily 6:00 a.m. workout routines in the facility fitness center and taking complete advantage of the fresh juices available in the cafeteria.

I crossed the room and sat in the only empty chair, facing Terry. His facial expression was not welcoming.

My stomach tightened.

This might not go so well.

Terry Scarborough was suited in crisp business attire—a navy suit, white-checked shirt, and blue-and-yellow tie. His hair was combed neatly to one side, a surreal shine emanating from a clearly new haircut. He had a square face that held sharp blue eyes, a thin mouth that looked like it had never seen a smile, and a slightly crooked nose. My eyes were drawn to his thick hands. I wasn't sure why it popped into my head, but the immediate thought was that he had the hands of a boxer. A schoolmarm would have been proud of his rigid, unrelenting posture.

Rebecca spoke up. "Terry, let me introduce you to Bill Matthews, who's been a critical piece to the growth and success of JHS. We'll have another meeting soon with his entire management team, where the finer details of his department can be discussed."

"I'm sorry," Terry impatiently responded, "but why can't we have that discussion now?"

If nothing else the man was direct. I suppose that would be good, as I wouldn't have to guess at what he wanted. What I really needed to convey was that I knew my business, but the trick would be trying to show him that fact without getting flustered.

"Fair enough," I piped in, starting my overview. "As I'm sure you know, JHS is facing a steady decline in revenue cycle performance, and we're having trouble maintaining net revenue levels, even though our patient population has remained roughly the same. This stagnation has been occurring for a few years now. Obviously, as vice president of revenue cycle management, I'm responsible for driving performance outcomes with the help of my team. We're currently working on an improvement strategy, but in the interim we're doing everything we can to improve outcomes . . ."

"I beg to differ," Terry interrupted.

"Excuse me?" Rebecca blurted out, incredulity in her voice.

"Prior to this meeting, I looked into performance metrics related to overall revenue cycle outcomes. They indicate that you're *not* doing everything you can. If you sincerely think you are, then I suspect you're either incompetent or just not very bright." Wow, and I thought he was direct before! Now my gut was getting more uncomfortable as it contorted several times.

As we talked more, I realized that Terry had already done a thorough review of the past year's revenue cycle trends. The issues at the top of the list are common in the industry: high avoidable write-offs, reduced reimbursement models, patient service revenue remaining relatively flat, and a steady decrease in average daily cash. Another red flag was the increase in billed accounts receivable (A/R), which indicated that too many claims were outstanding, and accounts were becoming harder and harder to resolve. This increase in account amount and volume was a clear indicator we were not efficiently resolving claims in error.

Terry narrated all of this information as if reading from a well-rehearsed script. Although his tone was matter-of-fact and mild, there was a slight undercurrent of condescension that was already threatening to give me a massive headache.

"Terry," Rebecca pleaded, "we know the problems. What we need to work on are clear solutions."

"That's a good idea, but I want to know what Bill has been doing to keep the pressure at bay. Do you have some solutions in mind that we can mull over now and discuss in detail at the next meeting?"

"Yes," I responded, "there are some initiatives that we plan on implementing over the coming months, but . . ."

"Yes? You need more funding? More time?"

"We need to integrate them into the current framework as seamlessly as possible. In a way that's acceptable for everyone and causes the least disruption."

"That's not how successful businesses operate. In the end it's all about performance, not how employees feel about new initiatives. Rebecca, you of all people should know this." He turned and looked at her as he finished the statement.

"We haven't historically run things the way you're suggesting, Terry. Ron spent years developing a culture of teamwork and consensus . . ."

"Well, not anymore." Terry interrupted her. "The Board brought me in with the clear objective of turning around JHS's underperforming financials. We can discuss how I intend to do that in the next meeting, whenever it will be held."

I felt an overwhelming compulsion to get out of the room. "Terry, if you would excuse me, I have a meeting with one of our bad debt vendors in a few minutes."

Terry stood up. "No problem, I'm already late for my next meeting. Let's make sure we stay on top of this. I'll talk to both of you later." With that he left the office, leaving both of us sitting there with stymied looks tattooed on our faces.

THE DEAL

April 8

MY MANAGEMENT TEAM was seated in the department conference room, hanging on to every word. I had been expecting my next meeting with Terry to be at least a week later, after he was done getting the lay of the land. To my surprise, it had been held the very next day.

"Okay," I told my team, "so the way things are, we have to come up with a solution very soon. Terry demands a solid plan in a month's time and results over the next eight months."

"Is that even feasible?" Kim asked. "Why the time limit?"

"Let's just say he's not like Ron."

"Well, what *is* he like?" Kim asked in a frustrated tone.

Thinking of that question, my mind wandered back to the second meeting—and the gut-wrenching feeling I experienced that day immediately returned.

▲▼▲

"Thank you for coming in early, Bill," Rebecca had begun. The three of us had been back in her office, and the mood was tense. "I've been thinking a lot on the root of our revenue cycle problems," she continued, "and Terry is right. We cannot afford to be in reaction mode anymore. We need to be more aggressive, and I want you pushing hard to improve results."

Interesting. I wondered if Terry had secretly come back to Rebecca's office the moment that I'd left, specifically to change her mind. I would not put it past him.

"Hey, I'm just as worried," I responded. "I'm sure we'll come up with something soon."

"Actually," Terry piped in, "I've already decided one thing that needs to be done to bring performance up to par." He pulled out a sheet of notes. "In addition to reviewing past revenue cycle outcomes, I also reviewed the performance of your management team. There has been a steady decline in quality over the years, and none of them are pulling their weight. By far the weakest link seems to be Mr. Daniels. You need to put him on a performance improvement plan."

I immediately felt myself getting hot. "Dave's been going through a bad divorce in the last year. A drop in his performance is to be expected, but I'm sure he'll bounce back."

"Bill, I need to ask you to leave your emotions out of this. I'm truly sorry if he's having domestic issues, but I have a very concrete policy of leaving personal problems outside of the workplace, and I expect employees to do that as well. Instead of defending a poorly performing member of your team, you need to come up with a contingency plan for replacing him."

"We don't fire employees when they need support. It's not the JHS way."

I looked at Rebecca for backup, but she just shrugged and said, "I'm sorry, Bill, but Terry's right. We can't afford to continue underperforming. I appreciate your loyalty to your team, but things need to change."

"Okay, okay . . ." I stammered, looking at the ceiling to buy myself some time. "Okay, let me offer this. I don't think Dave is the major source of our problems, but I do agree the organization has major issues. Give me some budget relief and eight months to solve this my way. If that doesn't work, then I will resign. Fair?"

Rebecca frowned and grimaced, but Terry was nodding with a look of satisfaction on his face. "I like a man who's confident and aggressive," he said, sticking out his open hand. "Eight months and not a day more. Deal?"

"Absolutely," I said, taking his hand, shaking it, and hoping that my palm hadn't turned to sweat. Eight months would take us into December. Which meant I might spend the holiday season preoccupied, to say the least. And Susan and the kids would pay the price.

▲▼▲

"So maybe we should conduct a comparative study analysis?" Kim suggested after I finished telling the story of my meeting to the team.

"Maybe, but JHS isn't like other health systems. Markets are different, available FTE talent is different, budgets are different. Just to name a few." I sighed. "Anyway, think of some workable options over the next few days, and we'll get back together and see what we've collectively come up with."

The foursome left quickly, already in an animated discussion about solutions by the time they reached the door. I guessed that everyone has a different way of running things, and this was mine, which had always worked for me. Hire good people, let them know what the needs are, and then let them do their job. Micromanagement was not something I liked to do.

It will work again this time. I hope. After all, my career now depends on it.

PURSUING THE PLAN

April 17

"**G**OOD MORNING, HON."

"Good morning. I'm surprised you're up," I said as I looked up from my laptop screen to see my lovely wife. It always makes me smile to see her early in the morning with messed-up hair and sleepy eyes.

Barefoot and still groggy from sleep, Susan walked over to the couch I sat on and began rubbing my shoulders. "You were up all night?"

"Nah, I went to sleep around two and woke up just as the sun was coming up. Sleep can wait until after the presentation's done and dusted." A big yawn escaped as I talked.

"Yeah, but you still need a fresh mind to perform your best."

"I know . . . but a fresh cup of coffee made by my beautiful wife would sure help."

"How many have you had so far?"

I smiled and held up my hands. "I've only had tea, I swear."

"Since you asked so nicely, come into the kitchen in fifteen minutes." She gave my shoulders one last squeeze before leaving the room. Normally I wouldn't ask her be at my beck and call, but today was a special circumstance. Today was the day I had to present a serious solution to the financial issues facing JHS. The entire Board would be at the meeting, so the pressure was high.

I'd spent the last few weeks reviewing several different aspects of our operations, first identifying all the issues we faced, and then brainstorming ideas with the team. Given my deal with Terry, I felt that the presentation would make or break my future at JHS.

I went back to the laptop, which showed a graph outlining performance of the department over the past years. Clicking an open Word doc, I resumed typing, listing all the external issues that had cropped up over the years that had affected departmental performance.

Ten minutes later, the heavenly smell of coffee wafted from the kitchen. I still had a few lines to type, which I would use as shorthand notes when giving the presentation, so I called, "Hon, can you bring my cup out here? I'm almost done with this."

As expected, Susan came to the doorway with a frown on her face. "No, Bill, take a break. I'm whipping up some breakfast as well."

"Really? Like what?"

"Like eggs, sausage, and toast. Now get up and come eat."

Knowing that arguing with my wife would be the wrong move, I stood up and closed my laptop. Although the idea of eating my favorite breakfast did lift my spirits, the pressure of the presentation clung to my mind. Once inside the kitchen, though, I saw Susan near the stove, cooking eggs and sausages in a big frying pan with her morning messy-bun hairdo, and I felt better already. I walked over to her and gently placed a kiss on the back of her neck.

She gave a quick giggle and asked, "Can you start four pieces of toast? Coffee's ready."

"Yes, ma'am."

The spread smelled awesome. In less than a minute, I cut the fried egg with a fork and had a bite with toast. Susan did the same, and immediately scrunched her nose in distaste. "Ugh, I forgot to season these."

"Tastes fine to me."

"Which proves your mind is definitely far away. Why don't you finish breakfast *without* thinking about work? After we're done, you can go back to your laptop and finish up. Then you can walk me through your presentation. Sound good?"

I nodded and we ate.

▲▼▲

After breakfast, I went back to the couch and started rummaging through a pile of files, looking for the notes I'd made during the night. A while later, Susan came in with yet another mug. From across the room, I smelled sweetness.

"Hot chocolate," she said. "I figured a little comfort food wouldn't hurt right about now."

"From Abbie's birthday jar in the fridge? Wow, you usually guard that with your life. I need to have life-changing meetings more often."

"Yeah, this will be the first one after the one where you met me."

I laughed at that. "Hon, you are amazing, and I'm lucky you didn't have any other options."

She ignored my lame joke and gestured to the laptop. "Okay, what do you have?"

"Well, the main issue Terry pointed out was that our traditional performance metrics aren't working anymore. I need to show the Board that the metrics *will* work with the new plan."

"And what's the new plan?"

I took a gulp of the hot chocolate. "Reassigning roles and positions. That way, the employees will get to learn and apply something new, so development of the staff will hopefully enable them to perform better and work more closely as a team."

"But what if those employees aren't equipped to handle the new roles?"

"We'll provide training."

"Which will take more time. Terry wants a solution that will produce results quickly, doesn't he?"

"Yes, but he is aware that making and implementing a completely new action plan will take months. Consequently, he and I agreed on eight months to turn things around."

"I may be wrong, but can you add new points to the action plan? From what you've already told me, I'm not sure he'll be impressed with this one. Also, shouldn't you also think about the other members of the Board's finance committee and how they might react?"

"Hmm . . . you're right. I've been so obsessed over proving to Terry that I can fix this, I completely forgot about convincing the other Board members."

"You still have time to redesign the presentation."

"Thanks hon."

"My absolute pleasure. Once you ace it, we'll celebrate."

"How?" I asked with a raised eyebrow.

"By taking the kids to the park."

My exasperated look made her laugh and of course I had to add, ". . . and then I'm sure we'll figure out something interesting to do afterwards."

▲▼▲

As I drove to the office, I could feel the warmth from the sun, which seemed to promise a nice day. I hoped it would be the same for me. Some apprehension regarding the presentation had been seeping into my mind, but thanks to Susan's help, I felt I'd covered all the important topics.

Unfortunately, and despite the fact that I was early, my usual spot at the parking lot was already taken. I tried not to think it was an ominous sign, but rather just a minor inconvenience. I could not let it get to me.

Once inside the building, I walked straight to the boardroom: the meeting was the first and most important thing on my agenda for the day. I entered the empty room and immediately hooked up my laptop to the very large TV at the end of the long table.

Then I walked to the water dispenser and refilled my bottle. I figured I would need it.

Ten minutes later, the room was full. All the members of the Board's finance committee had showed up, as well as Terry, who was the last to arrive.

"All right," I began. "Let me start by walking all of you through the underlying issues that have caused performance of the department to take a hit. The first one is obvious; employees aren't working at their full potential, despite the record showing that they can work hard and fast *and* correctly. After a brief study, I found that, though our employees are using the work queues assigned to them as they've been trained, each person uses those queues differently. It's making management oversight a problem, because we can't compare apples to apples for relative employee comparison.

"The second issue is at the very beginning of the process: payer rejection activity at the point of patient access. Over the past few years, we've seen a steady increase in insurance companies denying claim payments for coverage eligibility and clinical service authorization. With changes in contract plans, these are increasingly difficult issues to mitigate. One problem is that the payment rejections have grown only slightly every month, so they've been undetectable until we started specifically looking into it. Our reporting and tracking of this type of information is barely adequate and limits our ability to take action at the aggregated level that we receive the information. Last year, the numbers were actually within industry norms, but they've steadily picked up, and the trend is now exceedingly high."

Terry asked, "Do we have a plan to deal with these issues?"

"Good question, Terry. There are many reasons why this information is just now available. For one, changes in contracts with third-party payers, some of which have to do with the regular ones from the federal government and Medicare Advantage. Second, we don't have the required analytical tools to understand these issues in detail. As far as the plan, I'll circle back to that at the end the presentation."

"We're pressed for time, Bill. If you can present the action plan *now*, it would be appreciated. Does anyone object?" Terry looked around the table for concerns, but everyone was murmuring their support. Of him.

I began to feel increasingly anxious. "I could just jump right to the point, but I feel that knowing all of the background issues is essential for the plan of to be clear. Please bear with me."

I did not add: *Plus, I spent so much time making this presentation, and my team spent so much time gathering the data, I will NOT let Terry bully me into giving him what he wants.*

The next twenty minutes were spent walking the members of the finance committee through the numbers, issues, and dynamics of the situation. After I was done, I finally got to my point. "I propose we reassign employees to different roles within the department. This will allow us to fine-tune their skills and drive productivity to higher levels."

I expected many questions, even a barrage of concerns, so the resulting silence almost suffocated me.

"So . . . any thoughts?"

Terry's face clearly showed his frustration. "I don't think this is a solid plan of action. As a matter of fact, I don't think it is a plan at all."

"I second, Terry," said one of the Board members, City Councilperson Joan something-or-other. "The limited plan you've come up with just won't cut it. I can't see how this will give us the results we need."

"Look Bill, I'm not sure what type of leadership you're used to, but I'm a direct person," Terry continued. "There are many missing pieces to your strategy."

"Like what?" I asked a little too defensively.

"Well, for starters you haven't talked about putting actual controls in place. The Titanic will still sink no matter where you place your deckhands, and your department is a sinking ship. We need you to revisit your whole approach and come up with a more direct and aggressive one."

I tried to calm down and respond rationally. "Hmm, I didn't think about it from that angle, but that makes sense. Thank you. This feedback has been constructive, and I'm already formulating some thoughts on how to move forward." Frankly, I was hoping to not get fired on the spot.

In response to the obvious tension in the room, a round of uncomfortable chuckles rumbled from a few of the Board members present, and the meeting started to lose some formality as people started side conversations, which gave me a clear indication that my time was up. As I started to pack up my laptop, some of them stood and walked over to the food and coffee that had been laid out for the group. I hadn't noticed that Terry was waiting for me at the door.

"Bill, I know you spent a lot of energy to come up with this approach, but it's not going to get the results we need. Please try and understand the gravity of this situation. Things here are quite dire, and one thing I was brought here for was to turn it around. I need everyone on the bus, and it is moving quickly. Don't make it worse for yourself. There's always room for improvement."

"I understand. I'll revise the recommended course of action and bring back a better version."

With that, I walked out. What else could I have done? What else could I possibly do, except rework the approach that even I admitted was faulty? In that moment, all I really knew was that I couldn't wait for the day to end so I could go home to my wife and kids. As I looked up at the clock and saw that it was only 8:30 a.m., seeing my family felt like a lifetime from now.

WHAT ARE
THE METRICS?

Later that day

*T*HERE'S ALWAYS ROOM FOR IMPROVEMENT.

Terry's parting words kept reverberating in my mind on my way home. It was the end of a hard day, after an even harder week, but still executive management was not satisfied. I had to remind myself they don't pay me for effort but for results. I was a little lost at this point, frustrated beyond belief, and uncertain what the days ahead would bring for my team and me.

I was so distracted that I could not even appreciate the amazing landscape that I usually enjoyed along the drive. The fading sun gave off a few tendrils of light, bathing the clean streets of my neighborhood with gold and pink hues. Once I came within view of the house, I saw my boisterous children, whom I loved to death, playing on our little patch of front yard that was carefully tended by my wife. As always, she was sitting in a big chair. Mom and kids alike no doubt knew this was past the time "Daddio" usually came home.

I can't let her know about today. She helped me so much. She'll just be disappointed and upset.

I parked the car behind Susan's SUV and stepped out. The air was pleasant, as was the picture-perfect view in the yard. Given everything, I still smiled a bit at the SUV. Susan was not a minivan gal. Tough cookie, that one.

This is the reason I work so hard, I reminded myself. *I want to provide the best for my family, and I've done everything I can to achieve that. They deserve the best. This is WHY I must come up with a solution that satisfies Terry and the rest of the Board. The team in my department is also depending on ME to find a way out of this mess. There are too many people to let down if I fail. I need to get over today's setback and figure this out. It's time to move forward!*

Moving my thoughts to a temporary backseat, I walked to the front porch and picked up my youngest while kissing Susan on the cheek.

"How are they?"

"Oh, perfect little angels." She stood up, and signaled to the others that we were going to head into the house. "My sister wouldn't agree, though. She came by for a bit, brought homemade cookies, the crunchy oatmeal ones. She must have a sweet spot for you."

"I like anything your sister bakes, honey; I have no idea why she hasn't gone pro yet. She'd be amazing. We can invest if she needs help."

"Kelly knows that. She'll come to you when she's ready. By the way, will you be home this late every night? Just me being curious."

I caught the small amount of frustration in her voice as I fondly watched the children totter after their mother, squealing in delight at the prospect of dessert and apple juice—another ritual at the Matthewses' household. The rest of the evening was spent laughing at their antics and talking about how we spent our day. Thankfully, she didn't ask me too much about the meeting, so I didn't have to lie or frustrate her further.

▲▽▲

Later that night, I sat at the outdoor table on the patio, looking over a few files and switching between three open programs on the laptop. An empty coffee mug stood vigil beside my phone, the screen lighting up constantly with incoming messages. While I did my work, the rest of my team was doing theirs, so there was constant communication and follow-up in our text group.

More than once, I thanked God for technology. Trying to do this would've been so difficult if not for such advancements. I also knew that the solution to our problem was also tied to technology somehow. *There HAS to be a strategy that'll help take the performance of my department to a higher level,* I thought. *I just need to find it.*

I took a break to clean the kitchen and think. When I returned the laptop was in sleep mode.

I slowly gathered my files and scattered papers into some semblance of order. With a click on the space bar, it woke up showing the wallpaper image of the Pittsburgh Steelers. The phone's message light was still blinking; not surprisingly, two-dozen messages from the workgroup alone awaited. The last one had come from Dave and mentioned appropriate metrics.

"Hey boss, I've been thinking that using the normal industry metrics is the safe play. It could work, right? It's what everyone else uses."

I replied, "I know on the surface it might make sense to try and leverage a standard performance approach that has worked throughout the industry for years, but recently, things have changed dramatically. I've been cramming through some research on topics I've heard from industry leaders on webinars and at conferences. Stuff like advanced automation and augmented analytics, for example. When those types of tools are in play, the whole game changes. And I have to believe the measurements change with them. Let's discuss this further tomorrow."

Not wanting to continue the text message conversation this late in the day, I proofed it quickly, hit send, and put my phone on silent.

▲▽▲

The next morning, I found myself deep in thought about performance monitoring as my team settled into the conference room. All pending tasks for the day had been put off because we were now officially in crisis mode.

"Okay," I started, "so the value that key performance indicators, or KPIs, bring to the table is the definition of standard, and what we want from these indicators is for them to be something that allows us to compare across the industry. The main advantage of having strategic KPIs set in place is so we can determine a baseline to improve from, and then create an ongoing trend line to determine if we're going in the right direction. If so, life is fantastic. But what happens if the trend line isn't what we want? Then we need to ask how to shift performance to try to have an impact within a thirty-, sixty- or ninety-day cycle.

"One thing to consider is if we have enough discipline to use the industry standard metrics. The way I see it, if we really are going to manage our operations like every other organization, then we need to closely monitor five revenue cycle KPIs to drive high performance.

"The first is cost-to-collect, which is 'total revenue cycle cost divided by total patient services cash collected,' which is basically the amount of cash flow derived directly from a patient's clinical care and not related to items such as rent income or parking garage fees. Now total costs include patient access, patient financial services, health information management, outsourcing of account collection, benefits, subscription fees, software, and hard IT assets which, yes, are optional but still must be included."

"Just so we're all on the same page, how are you defining total cash?" Kim asked.

"Total cash includes patient-related settlements, payments, and bad debt recoveries. But since we only get summary reports from our outsourcing vendors . . ."

"Come on, Bill," Kim added. "I've worked with you long enough to know you're just going through the motions with this."

I paused slightly. "You're right. One, I believe they don't really tell the story of true performance deficiencies. Not those that identify root causes in a modern revenue cycle environment, anyway. And two, even if we continue using these industry standards, they're tied to the old way of doing business, and don't account for all the new technologies that could impact outcomes if deployed in a meaningful way.

"Think of just the departmental variables to consider here. Patient access, for example, covers core scheduling, preregistration functions, centralized registration, and various ambulatory admission functions. When it comes to patient financial services, it's not even clear whether some of these functions should be included or not. Most of these are used to compare to the industry, but they were created when the entire 'industry' was just individual hospitals. It's much more diverse now, and so many advances have been made, that what I think we need are measurements that compare us to ourselves, not others. Only then can we identify our internal opportunities for improvement."

"Wouldn't monitoring our accounts receivable performance help? If we keep the A/R levels in check that are greater than ninety days, isn't that a leading indicator of optimal performance?"

"Not really, because it could be controlled by write-offs and not cash collections. If the average daily cash isn't stable or rising, then the 'gross-to-net ratio' is decreasing. If GNR decreases as A/R also decreases, that puts us in the situation we're in now, poor financial performance. We have to find ways to improve both cash and GNR simultaneously—all while finding ways to take cost out of the process. 'Days in A/R' measures the average number of days it takes for an account to be adjudicated, not necessarily paid. Turnaround expectations and then the actual payment window vary by the payer. I've never been a fan of using A/R days to measure performance. Too many ways to manipulate the value.

"And even if we go by this approach, it doesn't help with the cost side of the equation. How can we make material changes in our cost curve with our current mode of operations? When we have to perform follow-up with each open account, and we have over eleven hundred work queues to manage, it's just too time-consuming and FTE intensive. I looked at the work queue summary report yesterday for the first time in a while—really looked at it. How does anyone manage over a thousand of these and control the work that gets completed? Ideally, we need to design something that doesn't only measure and track performance at an enterprise level, but also helps maintain some consistency at the employee level." I laughed. "One of my operations professors from college used to talk about 'paving goat paths,' meaning being really efficient at ineffective processes. That's what eleven hundred work queues feel like to me."

"So how do we get there?" Dave asked. "I'm struggling to see how we can do anything differently, given the tools we have available to us."

"You're absolutely correct. It's like we're playing darts blindfolded. We don't need to get efficient at the current game; we need to change the game entirely. For example, I've been thinking: what if we could track at a granular level the 'contribution per employee?' This would allow us to understand how much each job function and each employee provides in value to the overall operations. While it might not be technically a hundred percent accurate, this measurement would allow us to ballpark how well the staff perform. And at the very least it might allow us to evaluate staff doing similar work activities against each other's performance."

"Sounds like a great concept, but we're gonna need more than an idea to survive this thing." Kim, always the voice of reality, chimed in again.

"I know. I just feel like we're behind the eight ball right now. If we don't take a big step forward conceptually, we'll still just be randomly knocking balls around the table in eight months."

"Well, as the CEO, it's Terry's prerogative to shake things up. We just need to focus on our job, right?"

"Right," I responded, not wanting to let them know that my job was on the line.

▲▼▲

Later that night, I continued with my research. "This article says companies need to consider their short-term and long-term business goals before setting up any performance management solutions. And many methods can be chosen."

"Huh? What are you reading, honey?" Susan said while looking up from her latest reading material, a bestselling novel. As per our evening ritual, we were both sitting up in bed with glasses of red wine. I had finally told her about the disastrous meeting, and she was now insisting on being my sounding board 24/7.

"The first method listed is management by objectives; the second is measuring productivity quantitatively." I trailed off, not sure what to do with the information in front of me and afraid to upset her that I was thinking of work even as we relaxed. A lot of what I read sounded like my college business school classes. Neat concepts, but challenging to apply in a practical sense. Paving goat paths indeed. "Hon, a lot of this makes sense overall. The problem is getting the data I need. Nothing we have is granular enough."

Susan leaned over and read the rest of the paragraph on the screen. "Let me take a look at it. 'The quantitative method measures productivity by the number of parts or products an employed resource produces in a particular period, such as per hour, day, or month. This method works very well for small businesses, but even if you're managing large groups, this kind of performance measurement is simple and time-saving.' That sounds a little over complicated, doesn't it?"

"Possibly."

She continued reading. "'Productivity can be calculated with analytic software or on a spreadsheet, revealing the number of products an employee produces or contributes to in a given time period. Those numbers are then averaged out to reveal productivity gains or losses over time. Output can be measured either by the volume or quantity of products created or by the financial value of the product or service.'"

"Hmm," I said, pondering. "This is obviously written from a manufacturing standpoint, but a lot of it seems to be transferable to revenue cycle functions. Maybe there's something here. Measuring performance quantitatively might work—but throughput has to be considered."

"How does throughput impact what you do?" She was trying to be helpful, but I could tell this was too heavy for her this late in the day.

"Well, think about it this way. In order to improve an *individual's* productivity, you need to increase their throughput—take away things that slow them down and remove process bottlenecks. You also need to automate some of it, so that the *process* productivity is increased without adding FTEs, and therefore costs. Does that make sense? While this isn't the total answer, it 'feels' like the direction I need to take."

"You're welcome." Susan flashed me one of her patented smiles.

"I didn't say thank you."

"But you thought it!" She giggled to herself as if she had just said the funniest thing ever, and sleepily laid her head on my chest. "Babe, I hope you get through all of this in one piece. The kids and I miss you. Maybe you can come with us to Kelly's tomorrow?"

"Don't you have a brunch to go to?"

"It got postponed to Sunday. You can come now."

"I wouldn't miss your sister's famous apple pie for anything in the world."

The conversation flowed for a few more minutes until I turned off the lights. I listened to Susan's breathing becoming deeper as I stared sleeplessly at the ceiling. Not for the first time, I added to the list of my worries what I was doing to my home life while focused so much on work.

Tomorrow has to be a better day. At least that's what I promised myself.

WHY ARE METRICS IMPORTANT?

April 22

*I*T'S A BIT SIMPLISTIC, *but let's review the basics.*

I stood in front of the whiteboard in my office, writing down calculations. After being there with me all morning, Kim had just left to dig us up hot lunches. Years of MBA studies flashed through my mind as I jotted everything down.

A company's operating or cash conversion cycle shows the length of time it's taken to buy inventory, convert it into sales, and collect the revenue from those sales. "Accounts receivable" is an accounting term for this revenue, money that customers owe a company for purchases they make on credit.

Having a shorter operating cycle is typically better for a company because it allows for faster cash generation, which can then be used to pay bills or expand the business. The old saying that "a dollar today is worth more than a dollar tomorrow" very much holds true. How the operating cycle of a company is calculated is through an easy process known as the cash conversion cycle formula.

So, converting this into healthcare terms, the patient revenue generated by providing clinical care is billed to either the patient or the insurance company . . . and sometimes a portion to both, just to complicate the process. Unlike any other business, healthcare providers do not expect to be paid 100 percent of billed charges, and typically what patients and insurance companies do owe is determined by a convoluted three-way contracting arrangement between all parties, which makes the whole process incredibly difficult to administer. There is an accounting need to track the difference, or contractual adjustments. I like to call that the gross charge to net payment ratio, or GNR.

Stepping away from the whiteboard, I thought, *No wonder this gets so damn complicated.*

On the board, the words **A/R Days** were written in big, bold letters, followed by the respective calculations. How to calculate A/R Days? Take the total outstanding A/R and divide it by the *average daily revenue*, which is the past ninety days total billed charges divided by ninety.

My musings were broken by a voice at the door saying, "Boss, come on and eat while it's warm." As we sat down and prepared to dine, Kim looked over the completely filled whiteboard, an eyebrow raised at the mad scientist plans. "How do you intend to go about all this?" she asked, pointing a thumb at the board.

"It'll take some thought, but who knows? It might work. I just need to go over the figures again. It should only take a few hours at most." As I finished the sentence, I realized that not even I believed it.

"Why are you even going that route? What happened to trying to find non-industry standard metrics for calculating revenue cycle performance that we went over a few days ago?"

"I don't know . . . maybe." The whole process was starting to frustrate me and cause me to not trust my own instincts.

Kim stood up, grabbed the eraser, and wiped away all the writing, replacing it with: **Industry Standard Metrics**, followed by: 1) **A/R Days,** 2) **Cost to Collect,** and 3) **Unbilled Lags.**

"Okay." She began to slowly think out loud. "So, days in accounts receivable measures the average number of days it takes for an account to be resolved. Turnaround expectations vary by payer. The best practice is somewhere between thirty and forty days, depending on payer mix and specialty."

She paused slightly before continuing. "The only problem is, this can be manipulated by contractual adjustments and write-offs, so it doesn't have a one-to-one relationship to cash performance. It's actually a metric that was borrowed from other industries because it fit with accounting principles, not because it was accurate, but over time our entire industry started using low **A/R Days** as a primary justification for high performance."

I pointed to her next line, **Cost to Collect**. "For any given period, this is the ratio of adjusted operating expenses to patient services cash collections, expressed as a percentage."

"There's got to be an easier definition for what this is supposed to measure."

"Um, okay." I thought for a moment. "So, basically it's **Total Revenue Cycle Cost** divided by **Total Cash Collected**. The total costs include things like patient access and accounting, information management, outsourcing, benefits, subscription fees, software . . ."

"Hard IT costs?"

"Sure, that's an optional one. **Total Cash** includes patient-related settlements and payments, and bad debt recoveries. Basically, this is an overly complex way to monitor the investment it takes us to collect cash."

I directed our attention back to the whiteboard. "Last one. **Unbilled Receivables** is recognized revenue that has been accounted for, but for which the patient or insurance company hasn't yet received a claim. Basically, you've already provided the service to the patient, but you haven't billed them yet."

"So, it's just a cash flow issue?"

"Not always. There can be denials for things like coding errors, which impact GNR."

Soon the rest of the team had joined us for our regularly scheduled post-lunch conference, and I brought up the subject again to them. "Dave, how do we account for unbilled receivables?"

"We just include a section on the balance sheet for them. Unbilled receivables are usually counted towards total revenue even if an invoice hasn't been created. We can get them directly from the 'discharged, not final billed' report."

Kyle spoke up. "Boss, I've been thinking. A/R Days is our best bet. Yes, every financial metric is important in running a healthcare business, but tighter margins mean that the time between a patient's discharge and when payment is made is more important than ever. This directly impacts cash flow for JHS."

"So, the quicker the turnover in A/R, the less cash that we have to find somewhere else," Dave stated matter-of-factly.

"But more to the point, it's the metric used to monitor how quickly insurance companies process claims."

"There've been many times when insurance companies denied accounts or even payment," Dave reminded everyone, not for the first time.

"Yes," I nodded. "So the ultimate aim is to minimize the lag between claim submission and when the payment for those services is received. A/R days will measure how well we can complete this objective."

"So, how do we actually plan on reducing that lag time?" Ah, there was the Kim we were all used to, always moving toward action steps.

Everyone looked at Dave, who cleared his throat and said, "Well, first and foremost, we need to drop a clean and accurate claim to the payer as close to discharge as possible. The sooner this's completed, the sooner the account can be resolved."

"After it's been coded, Dave," Michelle added. "Nothing happens if we can't code the record."

"Also, payment from insurance companies is absolutely the biggest part of what we manage, isn't it? We have payment goals based on our experience with the major payers. From this history, we know we should be getting a certain amount of money each month. If we don't, we have metrics in place to find out where the issues are."

"A majority of accounts process and self-cure," I respond. "It's the accounts that get rejected that cause us issues." Everyone suddenly groaned and laughed, and I continued, "Yes, the dreaded 'claim not on file' or other hard denials. Those claims need to be reworked and resubmitted, which negatively impacts cash flow; and because they need work by someone here at the hospital, they increase our cost to collect too. And because not all of them eventually get approved for payment, we have to write some of them off, which decreases our annual net revenue. Denials are the bane of the industry."

"Why do you think I'm always on Kyle's case to mitigate the denials in patient access?" Dave said with perhaps a bit too much enthusiasm.

"Oh, here we go again," Kyle mumbled. "Don't let the facts get in the way of a good story, Dave."

"But Bill," interjected Kim. "These are the metrics we're already looking at every day. If they got us into this mess, I don't think they'll get us out just because we're now acknowledging that a denial write-off is as 'valuable' as a payment."

That revelation shocked the room to silence for a moment. "You really are convinced we need to look somewhere else?" I asked, trying to keep things moving.

"Kim makes sense," Kyle quipped. "But everybody in the industry is using these metrics, so why wouldn't they work for us too?"

"Maybe they aren't, and they don't know the difference?" I mused out loud.

Ever pragmatic, Dave chimed into the discussion again. "Maybe Terry's right. What if we look at other organizations of the same type and size as JHS, and see where they're doing better than us? This kind of comparison just might get us somewhere with our performance."

"Except for one thing; even if their numbers are better, we don't know what they're doing right to cause it. And there are so many variables at JHS that are different from other hospitals."

We spent the entire afternoon in the meeting, yet by the end we had exhausted several avenues without finding a solution. What was more frustrating was that the answer seemed to be right there at the tip of our understanding, but we were unable to grasp it. Back inside my office, I collapsed into my chair, starting to chew on my pen. I thought about how much I needed a break, but how that would not be coming until these issues were resolved.

A notification popped up in my email, a reminder for a revenue cycle conference happening in the area in three days, featuring some unique thought leaders in the industry. I went over the list of speakers for the conference, noted the venue and times, and recorded it all in my planner.

I knew it was going to be tough to fit in, but I also knew it was important. *With any luck,* I thought with a small chuckle, *I'll learn something new.*

THE McPHERSON PRINCIPLE

May 2nd

"**H**ONEY, KELLY WANTS TO KNOW if you want her to send some of the homemade jam you gorged on along with the bread slices," my wife said gently on the other end of the phone.

"Oh heck, yeah, I love your sister's jam. Also bring home some of her cinnamon bread if there's any left."

"I wish you could have stayed longer. Did you eat okay before you had to take off?"

"Yes, Susan, Kelly fixed the perfect 'grab n' go' sandwich for me. Tell her one more time that I said thanks."

"I will. When will you be home tonight?"

"I think by six or seven."

"All right. Have a good day, luv." And with that, she hung up the line.

I clicked off the speakerphone and turned the car radio's volume higher. It was on a country station that was belting out old tunes from Eric Church and Jason Aldean, with a bit of Blake Shelton thrown into the mix. I was heading towards the Innovation in Healthcare Conference, which was being held in a five-star hotel downtown, twenty minutes from my suburban home.

Let's just hope the conference is worth it, I thought . . . *I don't want to waste an entire Saturday when I should be spending my day off with the family.*

I arrived at the venue in no time at all, thanks to less than normal traffic, as well as my less than great singing with the radio that allowed the time to pass. I found a good spot, parked the car, and walked inside. Less than five minutes later, I was sitting in a padded chair in the fairly crowded room, which I judged to hold a few hundred, waiting for the first panel to begin. I browsed through a pamphlet that had been on the seat. The contents covered a detailed agenda as well as a list of speakers. I wondered if I had heard any of them before.

Hmm, Ben Gordon is new. Haven't heard him. Jim Bolton, Neal Harris, Indira Sethi, Doug Lewis, Max Pullman . . . . Interesting lineup.

Just then a suited man walked to the podium on the slightly raised stage at the front of the room.

"Good day everyone. My name is Steve Polonsky, and I welcome you to the fifth annual Innovation in Health Conference. For those of you who attended last year, we have a similar format. I will introduce the different panels that will be discussing various topics throughout the day, and then each speaker will cover a set group of items. First, though, we'd like to start with a word from our chapter president, through whose efforts this has been possible. Mr. Artie Andrews, would you come to the stage please?"

A man in his late fifties walked up and was handed the mic. He gave an uninspiring speech about innovation being the key element in healthcare performance, primarily related to the various technology options in today's revenue cycle operations sector. I mostly tuned it out.

After he was done, the first speaker, Ben Gordon, was invited to the stage. He was a short man with a balding head, huge wire-rimmed glasses, and a long face.

"Good morning. Thank you for having me today. As a way of introduction, I'll just mention that I have based my entire career on revenue cycle performance, so I'm hoping I can add some value to your day. With that, let's get started . . ."

The problem with Ben was the same one with the next several speakers who took the stage: there were some novel approaches, but nothing new was covered, just the same concepts that I already knew about, with some minor updated spin to reflect the latest trendy piece of technology.

Is there truly nothing innovative anymore in this industry? At this rate, I'm not going to find anything that will help solve my problems. What a waste of time. Maybe I should just give up, go to the hotel bar, have a drink or two, and call Susan? It's been so long since we had a date night, just the two of us. Maybe I can talk her into coming over?

I took my phone out, ready to dial Susan's number, now paying only half-attention to the stage, where the presenter was announcing the name of the next speaker to grace the stage after a short break.

"Doug Lewis, who's an innovation consultant, will be coming on next. He'll talk about the McPherson Principle, which encompasses new ways to measure success and drive operational performance improvement. Be back in your seats in ten minutes, please, so we can begin the session on time. Thank you."

I stood up with the rest of the attendees. I walked towards the refreshments table, waited in line, and made small (very small) talk with two or three other attendees. When the line finally receded I picked up a small water bottle and left the room. Outside in the hallway, I dialed my wife. She picked up on the fourth ring.

"Hey hon, the conference is mostly a bust," I said as quietly as possible. "But the hotel is nice, so I was thinking maybe you could drop the kids off at your sister's and come up here? Maybe we can sit and talk at the bar or have a nice dinner."

"Sorry to hear about the conference, but sure, honey, I'll ask Kelly. I'd love to spend time with just us . . . It's last minute, but hopefully she can help us out. I'll shoot you a text once I get an answer."

The next session was about to start, so I went back to my seat. And Doug Lewis walked to the stage. He was a tall man, with a signature "executive type" hairstyle peppered with a few silver strands. His face was jovial looking, as if anything could bring a smile to his lips. I tried to focus on what he was saying, but my mind was on the text that I was waiting for.

Someone in the audience commented on the speaker's tie being a bit too colorful, at which he laughed, a booming sound that made me look up at the stage.

"What is innovation in healthcare?" Doug then continued. "It's about not following the herd but more in line with thinking differently and trusting your instincts when it comes to making decisions. Think of it like taking on new initiatives and deploying better tools to change the rules of the game. And to be sure, there *are* things that change the rules of the game in healthcare. Today I will be talking about one of them, the McPherson Principle. You may have not heard of it . . ."

The rest of his words faded away when the phone in my hand vibrated once. I looked down to see a message from Susan:

Kelly is game. I'll be there in 30.

Gladdened, I leaned back and prepared to immerse myself in Doug's presentation, when just a few seconds later the phone vibrated again.

Small delay, but ETA 15 min.

What? How did she make such fast progress? Looking at the timestamps, I realized that the messages were being delivered to me late, and that Susan was probably walking in the front door at that moment. I stood up and began to walk outside, only glancing back one last time at the man still on the stage.

▲▼▲

"Another Woodford, sir?"

"Yes please, neat. And another merlot for my wife, I think."

"Coming right up."

The bartender slid a freshly filled bowl of mini-pretzels to me before getting busy pouring the drink. With Susan in the ladies' room, I took the time to observe the other patrons in this area of the bar. Well-dressed men and women sat around, phones or books in hand. I was startled at the sound of a man's laugh coming from behind me, which was followed by him sitting down next to me and ordering a "Jack and Coke."

Our eyes met and suddenly I remembered who he was. "Oh, hello," I said. "The McPherson Principle, right? My name's Bill Matthews. I was in the audience."

"Oh yes," he said, shaking my hand. "I hope it helped you."

"To be honest, I got called away right after you started."

"So, you've heard of the McPherson Principle?"

"I haven't, actually. Any chance for a quick recap?"

He laughed. "I'd love to, but I leave in fifteen minutes, and it's a much longer conversation than that."

"Just my luck. I'm in a real bind at work with our revenue cycle operations, and it sounded like that's exactly what you were addressing."

"Tell you what, Bill," he said, giving me his card. "Here is a quick overview to get you started. The McPherson Principle at its core is about thinking differently. Conceptually applying new thoughts to old problems. Tactically, it's about leveraging the manufacturing philosophy called 'Theory of Constraints.' Are you familiar with it? Basically, it's about the speed of account processing. How can we get accounts through faster without human interaction? By focusing on throughput, healthcare organizations can vastly improve financial outcomes. In a nutshell, it consists of implementing a strategy of daily, incremental improvements that over a short period of time enable significant improvements. The strategy is supported by using three metrics that will give clear guidance where the incremental improvements should come from. Those metrics are process effectiveness, operational efficiency, and employee performance. Finally, leveraging advance technology, like augmented analytics, allows you to continue refinement of activities and results over time, as well as improve sustainability of those results."

"Wow, that's a mouthful," I said with a smirk on my face.

"Once you're home, give me a call, and we'll set a time to discuss how to implement, measure, and accomplish those three objectives in more detail."

"Wow, thank you so much . . ."

"My pleasure. Talk to you soon."

As I watched the man walking away, I thought, *This has to be a good sign. Or he was a snake oil salesman and I was about to be played?* But what choice did I have but to at least listen?

MAKING SENSE

May 12

AFTER RETURNING TO THE DAILY GRIND, Doug and I exchanged a few emails but we hadn't been able to sync up calendars yet to really discuss my situation. Then, one day about a week after the conference, I was coming back to my office after lunch and received an email from Rebecca, asking me to stop by her office with my latest progress report as soon as possible. When I did, I found her standing beside a bookshelf with an open book in her hands. "Hi, Bill, how are you?" she asked, then invited me in.

"Here's the report," I said. "It's more or less the same thing we've been going through for the past few days. I did recently discover some potential new insights at the conference I attended, but I haven't had time yet to integrate them into my final plan."

"It's all right, Bill. I'm sure whatever's inside the report will help."

Given the urgency in her email, Rebecca seemed strangely disinterested in the meeting. I turned to leave, but then decided to forge ahead.

"Rebecca, I wanted to give you a heads-up regarding a path I might take. I've become aware of a concept related to advanced revenue cycle management called the McPherson Principle."

"Interesting. Did you learn about it at the conference?"

"I heard about the building blocks of the concept there, but I need to work it around myself to make more sense out of it, and to figure out how to apply it to our environment. For example, I've been researching in the evenings, and one important aspect is a measurement called the process effectiveness ratio (PER), which can possibly increase the output of the revenue cycle overall. The PER basically measures the process performance of specified business and payer requirements. Every process should have a purpose that includes a strong value proposition for the activity involved. This process includes defining the preferred end state, the problem solved by the process, and how it does so."

"Interesting," she responded distractedly. "Well, just keep me in the loop."

I wanted to talk through it more with her to help myself, but I could tell that I had been dismissed. Rebecca's inattention to what I was saying made me think about my place in the company. It was difficult for me to imagine leaving JHS, especially after giving so many years of my life to the growth of the hospital; but clearly, I was reaching a point where I was going to be forced to make some hard decisions.

Going back to my office, I decided to make some calls to a few recruiter contacts who would know about good opportunities elsewhere. The thought didn't make me happy.

▲▼▲

"You've been cooped up inside for hours on that laptop, Bill. Come outside for a bit. It's such beautiful weather."

Susan gave me a wistful smile and closed the sliding door, leaving me alone again with my thoughts. It had been a few days since my meeting with Rebecca, and officially a month since my first disastrous encounter with Terry, and I still hadn't gotten any further no matter how many Google searches I performed on the McPherson Principle. I went back to the open files on my laptop, reviewing the information I had compiled for the umpteenth time.

Why am I so lost? I need to find something to help, and this information is interesting, but all it leads me to are more questions. Everything I've found is at such a high level that it isn't very helpful. How do I implement the ratios that Doug outlined when I can't even understand what the actual formulas are? The principle Doug explained might be easy in theory, but in practice it isn't. What am I doing wrong?

I went over the operational efficiency ratio (OER) again based on what little information I could find on the internet. This would be so much easier if I could just talk to Doug, but since he was out of the country I was left to try and figure it out myself. Regardless, the OER consisted of the number of new accounts in the discharged, not final billed (DNFB) category, divided by the number of DNFB accounts that have been released; added to the number of new accounts in the aged trial balance (ATB) category, divided by the number of resolved ATB accounts . . .

$$OER = \frac{\# \ new \ DNFB}{\# \ released \ DNFB} + \frac{\# \ new \ ATB}{\# \ resolved \ ATB}$$

This ratio should be less than 2; if it was larger, it meant the inflows are greater than the outflows, and therefore backlogs would form, resulting in a decrease of overall cash related to the collection of accounts. It was an interesting concept, if nothing else, especially as outpatient volumes increase and inpatient volumes decrease.

I realized that the process effectiveness ratio (PER) formula was simpler:

PER = First Pass Rejection Volume / Total Claims

This ratio should be less than 2 percent. If greater, then significant process breakdowns existed, and they'd have a material impact on FTE costs to rework errors; if less, then there should be a direct impact on operating cost reduction, increased throughput, and cash flow improvement.

Then came the employee performance ratio, or EPR. After flipping through the published presentation material from Doug's talk, he had mentioned this should work for all financially driven job functions within the revenue cycle—patient access preregistration, medical records coding, patient financial services billing, and follow-up. The productivity factor changed by work activity. The formula was a little more complicated and was measured in the following way:

Step 1:   *(# of Resolution Actions) + (# of Processing Actions × .25) = Effectiveness Score*

Step 2:   *(Effectiveness Score / Performance Base) × 100 = Employee Performance Ratio*

This ensured that staff remained focused on what was important instead of what was expedient, which was what our old productivity model measured. According to an email I'd received from Doug in which he'd been able to share some concrete information, the various performance base number of activities performed, such as accounts worked, by each functional group were as follows:

1. Preregistration: 40
2. Coding:
    a. Inpatient: 20
    b. Observation: 14
    c. Ambulatory Surgery: 30
    d. Outpatient: 155
    e. Emergency Room: 175
3. Billing: 140
4. Third Party Follow-up: 50

Looking over the formulas and numbers, I felt more confused than when I started. Opening the contact list in my phone, I searched for Doug's number and pressed the dial key. He was probably my only hope in understanding the ratios and coming up with a solution, so I could fix the problems in my department and the health system . . . and not have to take another job. I just hoped he was free for a detailed discussion. I really needed him to explain how these metrics had proven to be useful in practice!

THE TWO KEYS

May 15

WHEN I FINALLY COULD REACH Doug by phone and I explained my situation, he agreed that implementation could be particularly tricky when it came to the McPherson Principle.

"What I want you to think about," he said, "is efficiency and effectiveness from an operational standpoint. Where can you leverage both workflow and automation efficiency to dramatically improve results? Another concept to think about is the power of one percent. If you improve something 1 percent each day, in six months you'll have a dramatic change for the better. That's the core of the McPherson Principle; incremental changes on a daily basis but using the right measurements to track your progress."

After finishing the call, I opened my laptop and began my research from scratch. Half an hour later, I stumbled across something truly interesting.

Robotic Process Automation. I was curious.

At first glance, it seemed to involve a technology that allows anyone to configure computer software to emulate and automate repetitive processes. Basically, it seemed to be a bot that emulates a human interacting within a digital system to execute a business process. RPA—as it's called—utilizes the user interface to capture data and manipulate applications, *just like humans do.* The process interprets, triggers responses, and communicates with other systems to perform a vast variety of repetitive tasks. Even more important, RPA is substantially *better than humans,* as the software robot never sleeps, makes zero mistakes, and doesn't need a coffee break.

I read the complete page on RPA and contemplated various applications.

This sounds better than useful, I decided, *especially when considering the 1 percent improvement concept. Enabling RPA would not only transform and streamline our workflow, but it would route work with exception codes to our staff for human review. This could free up FTE resources from wasted time with mind-numbing repetitive work.*

And it could be one of the things that saves me.

There was a knock on my doorframe, and I looked up to see Dave. "Hey, Bill. You missed Mike's birthday."

"Any cake left?"

"Yeah, I think there's still some in the fridge. What are you working on?"

I shared my notes on RPA with him, and he nodded. "And it's a strange coincidence," Dave said. "The other day I was reading about intelligent scripting, which seems pretty similar. It's sometimes described as low-grade process automation. It's been around forever. Remember years ago when we used scripting to post payments, before we started getting electronic 835 remittances? It's that but with some artificial intelligence characteristics. The nice part is that it can be implemented fairly quickly—like in just a few weeks."

I started to realize that there was a link between the McPherson Principle, the power of one percent, and various automation techniques, even if Dave sounded like a robot himself when trying to describe it, that last thought causing a sly smile to sneak across my face.

"Boss, something funny?"

"Nothing at all, Davebot. Now, let's go see if any of that cake is left."

THE CONNECTION

May 18

"OKAY, CAN YOU HELP ME understand the throughput ratio?" Kim asked the next day when I was having a brainstorming session with her. "Explain it again, please."

"It's a performance measuring tool," I replied. "It's often used when implementing a system of management based on the Theory of Constraints. It's also sometimes called the 'flow rate'. The ratio can be calculated per item, batch, or product line. Essentially, the ratio helps to measure the movements of inputs and outputs within the process. It indicates how successful the overall business is, based on efficiency of all the departments. Optimizing throughput levels is often the key driver in maximizing a company's revenue."

I walked over and started writing on the whiteboard. "The manufacturing formula for this ratio is . . ." I wrote **inventory = throughput × flow time** on the board.

"Manufacturing? But where can we apply it?"

"Ah, that's the million-dollar question. It's applied in three places, first being the inventory—but be careful with the definition. In accounting, *inventory* includes products or services that are waiting to be sold; but in operations management, it includes all the units within the entire system. The second place it's applied is the flow rate *throughput*, which is the rate at which the units go through the process. This rate is measured in time, such as units per minute, for example. The last one is *flow time*, which is the time that units spend in the business process from beginning to end.

"Consider a company that manufactures chairs. The management wants to increase profits by improving the operations process, so it decides to find out what the company's current throughput is. If one hundred chairs are held in inventory, and the average time from production to selling is five days . . ." I wrote on the whiteboard:

$$R = 100 \text{ chairs}/5 \text{ days}$$

". . . it can be stated that daily throughput is twenty chairs."

"So," Kim said with a look of serious confusion, "maybe we just need to look at solutions that offer improved account processing?"

I could see she still wasn't grasping what I was trying to say, but I could also feel myself on the tip of a breakthrough. "Okay, maybe this will help. Medical Records Coding might be the easiest example. Inventory would be the accounts waiting to be coded, and finished products would be coded accounts ready to send to a payer. Now, for inpatient accounts, we should average around twenty-five a day per coder. So, if we had one coder and one hundred accounts waiting, our throughput rate of twenty-five a day would take five days to move our backlog to finished product, unless we changed our throughput."

Kim paused for a moment, looking at the whiteboard, then said, "The only way I see this really working is to redesign our processes to be more consistent across job functions, and to group employees in categories where they're doing similar functions. Essentially codifying business processes so we can automate some activities, but also reducing variability when staff perform their work. Theoretically, it would result in faster cycle time and fewer errors in revenue cycle processes. But can this automation technology be used in *our* business model? Especially considering the thousand or so work queues for Revenue Cycle alone?"

"That's why I wanted to discuss this with you. The more I learn about the McPherson Principle, the more I realize we need new tools to make significant progress." I turned back to the whiteboard. "Okay, so the definition of process efficiency is 'the amount of effort or input required to produce a service or product,' and the operational efficiency ratio tells us how efficient the account throughput is, once clinical services are performed. So what's the best way to measure account throughput? I'm thinking we're just talking about the throughput when we submit a claim to the insurance companies."

"No, Bill. If you read the definition again, it states 'once clinical services are performed,' so I would think it includes unbilled as well."

"Oh yeah, right. So throughput is about moving accounts through the gates of a process. The gates in this instance are discharged not final billed, final billed not sent, which are those accounts held in the claim scrubber, and accounts receivable. When asked Doug for clarification, he shot me a quick email with a formula that now makes more sense." I wrote it on the board:

$$OER = \frac{\# \ new \ DNFB}{\# \ released \ DNFB} + \frac{\# \ new \ A/R}{\# \ resolved \ A/R}$$

"But how is this different than A/R Days?" Kim asked.

"Good question. A/R Days measures how fast we're moving *money* through the system, while OER measures how fast we're moving *accounts* through the system. I wonder why Doug is more focused on volume instead of dollars." I paused. "Wait, could this have something to do with the concept of 'next most valuable' that he also mentioned in his message? If I have business rules in place that dictate that the next piece of work a staff member will perform has the highest value to the organization, then I don't need to focus on the dollar amount, as it will take care of itself. What I need to focus on is volume, because that's where we'll make gains—especially when automation and RPA are factored in. So the next logical question, I suppose, is whether RPA can actually be applied to this process."

"Absolutely," Kim replied. "Applying robotic process automation would further reduce staff errors, which has a direct effect on operational efficiency. Now, what about employee performance ratio? We need to know how to make people better at their jobs."

"Can't we just deploy training on a departmental level? Or maybe bring in new people?" I ask.

"Not really, because right now we have no way of knowing the areas where people are underperforming. We need a way to measure the two related but independent factors—how much work employees perform, and how well they do it. Productivity versus effectiveness. I read the other day that improving productivity is considered an incremental improvement, but that effectiveness is an exponential improvement. That makes it a more important metric, but also much more difficult to develop and measure."

"So how do we measure EPR?"

"A few days ago I saw an article about a collection agency that monitors the actions taken by their representatives, and how they define an action as 'high quality' when it's one that moves their work to the next appropriate step for resolving the account."

"I like that. So, the definition of 'effective' means taking the next most appropriate action to complete the task at hand, regardless of what your job function is."

We both sat back for a few minutes to let that sink in. Could it really be that simple?

In her typical maddening but welcome fashion, Kim quickly burst my bubble. "I do think you're right on the definition, Bill, but measuring that would be almost impossible with the tools we currently have available."

"What if we make securing appropriate tools a requirement for our new solution? Do you think that might work?"

"Possibly . . ." Kim said hesitantly.

"I'll take that," I said, laughing. "So, we've defined EPR and figured out an option to hopefully measure it. But without improving an employee's capabilities, we're just paving the goat path all over again." Kim had already heard me use the term many, many times. By now she knew that paving a goat path referred to speeding up a broken process so that all you really accomplished was making mistakes faster than someone would normally.

"I think training is essential to driving peak employee performance, much more than bringing in new people. We definitely need to modernize our training materials and approach."

"What do you think about combining employee productivity with robotic automation?"

"I like it! Let's develop a plan to include automation at least for patient access and patient financial services where we can. The question is, what processes?"

"How about if we pick the two largest denial patterns for both teams?"

"So essentially we're talking about checking insurance eligibility and obtaining treatment authorization on the front end and determining claim status as well as administrative billing corrections on the back end."

I was beginning to believe in the old adage about light being at the end of the tunnel, but then remembered that could also be a train instead of salvation.

Next, we moved on to the process effectiveness ratio. "This one is easier to understand," I said, writing it on the board:

(Volume of First Pass Payer Rejections / Total Patient Accounts)

"Essentially, this is a measurement of how effective our processes are at producing positive results. But the question is, do 'first pass rejections' include primary and secondary claims or just primary?"

"Considering it's a 'process' measurement," Kim offered, "wouldn't it include both, as any rejection is cause for rework?"

"Yep, that makes sense." I took a long pause. "Now if we can just figure out how to apply it."

TWO WEEKS

A FEW DAYS LATER I was summoned yet again to Rebecca's office. When I arrived, I learned Terry was there too, along with a man I recognized from the Board meeting. A stack of reports was scattered on the table, and from the looks of the covers, they were all my reports on the performance metrics.

This doesn't look good.

"Jim," Rebecca said to the other man, "I think you remember Bill? He's presented at a few finance committee meetings. Bill, this is Jim Murphy, who heads the finance committee."

"Yes, I remember Bill. How have you been?"

"Doing well, other than this revenue cycle performance solution that continues to elude me." I suddenly felt very nervous.

"That's why I had Rebecca call you," Terry said. "Jim might be able to help us with the problems your department has been facing. I've been picking his brain for a while now, considering that his role on the Board is to provide financial guidance."

"Ah, Terry, I appreciate your confidence," Jim replied, "but I'm coming at this as much from a point of ignorance as from knowledge. My background's in banking, which is so much different than healthcare."

"Any extra help is welcome . . ." I felt compelled to say, but maybe a little too quickly. Now that the Board was involved with this whole thing, it couldn't help but become a political nightmare.

"Regardless, Bill," Terry continued, "I need an update on the performance improvement plan we talked about a month ago. Any progress?"

I dove into a brief overview of what my team had recently concluded, how the normal metrics shared in the monthly performance revenue report would no longer apply to the business operational framework, assuming some of our future ideas worked out.

Terry sighed. "I was hoping you'd made more progress."

I gave an apologetic chuckle. "I'm working from the old saying 'don't steal small money.'" Upon seeing their blank faces, I explained further. "I'm really trying to concentrate on the big picture here, not suggest quick stopgap measures."

Terry paused then turned back to Rebecca. "So, if there's nothing else . . ."

With that, I got up and walked to the door. As I left the administrative corridor, I paused outside the door overheard them resuming the conversation. "What do you think, Rebecca?" Terry was saying. "Can he pull through?"

"I think so. Remember that first meeting with him? There's been such a change since then."

"What do you think, Jim?"

"I think he's winging it."

Well, there you have it. The pressure is continuing to mount.

DATA REVELATION

Later that day

IT HAD BEEN TEN MINUTES since I'd started my car and begun driving home from work, and my mind was drifting. I had been pulled into one fire after another today, making strategic thinking even harder than usual. After a lot of time and the combined effort of everyone, it looked as if we were finally getting our heads wrapped around the measurements Doug had exposed us to; but applying them was something we still hadn't quite figured out, or even if such a thing was possible.

Unknowingly, but maybe instinctively, I turned the car into an area I had been to many times before. The Tropicana, my favorite dive bar, loomed ahead in the distance. So many good memories attached with this place—my first date with Susan, countless hangouts with college friends before and after graduating, becoming one of the "regulars," and then getting special treatment from the bartenders once I had started making enough money to become a good tipper.

As I entered the bar, I immediately noticed that it was almost empty, with just a few others sitting at tables, quietly sipping beverages. The interior of the Trop is a little dingy and worn out; the only remotely modern item in the place is the jukebox, which streams music from the internet and can be activated from your phone. Unfortunately, it was playing pop music when I walked in.

Pop music at a country bar? What blasphemy is this?

I pulled out my phone, bought ten dollars in credits, and changed the music to Eric Church. Then I sat down and asked the bartender Donna for a cold beer and spare pen and paper. When she'd complied with the pen and paper, I wrote down *How to Really Measure Operations*, followed by three question marks. My mind was a whirl of activity, thinking of the many different ways this could be achieved.

As I put down the pen and waited for the beer, a thought came out of nowhere: *What if I had joined the Marines as I'd originally wanted?* I thought back to that night decades ago, when I first told my college buddies Steve and Bryan about my change of plans.

"You guys know the situation," I'd said to them. "I don't have the luxury of waiting. I'm out of school now and can't afford to sit at home and be a mooch. My mom is a single parent who almost killed herself to pay for my schooling. I told myself I was going to join the Marines if I didn't get a job offer in the next week, and yesterday this small hospital contacted me about a systems analyst position."

A few weeks later, I was halfway across the state and starting the new job. The pay was barely livable, but there were several opportunities to grow. I pushed myself to learn the systems side of operations, but also spent my spare time learning how the processes and people interacted. Soon I had developed a natural eye for "fixing" problems, a trait that helped me climb the management ladder.

The beer arrived; I took a long, cold sip and wondered about the differences between then and now.

How much has changed today, in terms of the work JHS does? And yet the industry is still measuring everything exactly the same way it was being done twenty years ago! I remember a time when clerks would still type UB82 claim forms on an electric typewriter and physically mail them to insurance companies. Reports would literally be printed on paper from a mainframe computer the size of a room.

Suddenly, it was as if a lightbulb had switched on above my head. *Of course. Data is the key.* Was it possible that the methods I had used years ago to extract and manipulate mainframe data could still be a practical approach? How is it that back then we used print image files from the mainframe system reports, downloaded them as files, wrote GW-Basic code, extracted that data, and somehow still ended up with more powerful information than we're able to get now?

The revelation was so exciting that I didn't even realize how long I had been there, and I almost spit out my beer when I took another sip and learned that it was now room temperature. I dropped a $20 bill on the bar and waved goodbye to Donna, excitedly heading back to my car.

Coming to the Trop had been a good idea.

RPA AND DATA

That evening

WAITING FOR THE TRAFFIC LIGHT to turn green, I sat in the car and pondered the discoveries I'd made in the past hour. Leveraging data not only to enhance operational visibility, but also from a workflow perspective, was the first and foremost priority for us to find a solution to developing an advanced revenue cycle ecosystem.

How to do it was the question.

We're going to need good data, and to start we need to define "good data." Mostly, good data should provide the ability to sift through all the noise, and then quickly identify current and future opportunities that are relevant to our performance; we also need to be able to apply that data against business rules to prioritize work activities. What "good data" looks like requires an understanding of how the data should be used, what decisions need to be made, what work that information will help improve, and which actions or process will be supported.

The green light changed, yet I was so involved in these ruminations that I didn't notice. A few honks from cars behind me conveyed the message quickly, and I sped across the intersection. My mind was racing just as fast.

Assuming we get the right data, the next question is how we can make that data work for us in an actionable way. How can we make it work to support revenue goals? And I don't mean having something with red, green, and yellow indicators. I mean really actionable!

Thinking about the revenue goals of JHS, my mind went to one of the speakers at the conference who'd explained that, in most cases, key business functions such as clinical departments, accounts payable, finance, and information technology are already collecting data sets from their tactical and day-to-day operations. Although organizations are increasingly fluent about how to combine internally collected data sets such as these that support strategic initiatives, departmental solutions, and general analytic deployments, they have a long way to go when it comes to leveraging data about the functions in which they perform daily operations and how it directly affects workflow. High functioning and successful organizations usually rely on "solid, granular data" to help them with strategic planning as well as with tactical execution.

Which brings me to the big question, I thought. *How do I utilize data and implement a solution that improves my situation? It feels as if I've been repeating this question again and again without coming up with any concrete answers. There are many approaches to doing this; the first I can remember from early in my career was service line analysis. This approach helps identify which offerings or services could be discontinued with minimal impact to the hospital and the community, and which have considerable growth potential. This type of analysis weighs variables that are most critical to an organization—revenue, profit margins, customer impact—when it comes to driving decisions that both streamline services and enhance profitability . . .*

Hold on a second.

I knew there was more swimming in my brain. I waited for it to coalesce into something tangible. That's when I recalled an article I'd read in *Business Digest* during my research.

The article discussed robotic process automation and the use of data in general terms. So . . . would it be possible for us to combine data and RPA, with the appropriate business rules, to improve performance? Now, data shouldn't be thought of as just an analytic asset. Data is also a process enabler. If we could use data to help in the "performance" of tasks as well as to analyze the processes, then we could possibly make a large leap forward.

Holy cow, this is significant!

Another honk reminded me that I was still in the car and should probably pay better attention to my driving. I tried to focus on getting home safe and sound, but unfortunately, I couldn't help but think back to the conference, and the numerous articles I'd read about RPA.

I knew that this could be a big part of the answer.

Everyone always seems to be talking about the "process" side of RPA, but what about the "data" side? Once I'm home, I'll try to find the article I read about this the other day. I know there's more material on RPA available on the internet. After all, a lot of businesses have begun to integrate new technologies into their operations—it's a wonder JHS didn't think of it. Maybe that is the reason why we're in this bind.

Later that night, I helped clean up the kitchen. It had been a nice evening, and dinner was amazing as always. While it might seem basic to some foodies, when Susan made hamburger, gravy, mashed potatoes, and corn, I would fight an entire army of zombies just to get to the table. That night, the kids were lively and ate their meals without any fuss, and Susan was looking lovely.

How I lucked out with her, I'll never understand. She's the perfect life partner. Now if I could just figure out the work half of my life . . .

Feeling relaxed for the first time in a while, I went to the modest bar area next to our kitchen and poured two glasses of bourbon. Taking a firm hold on both, I walked to our bedroom.

"Hey, hon, special delivery."

Susan smiled. "Are you trying to take advantage of me?"

"Who, me?"

She rolled her eyes but reached out, took her glass, and turned back to her open laptop. Before she'd taken early retirement to "stay home" with the kids, she'd been a school math teacher from the same school our oldest now attended. Although it was summer break, she liked to spend time helping students find volunteering opportunities and part-time jobs.

Glancing my way, Susan asked, "Seriously, babe, how long will you be up? I'm getting a little bored going to sleep by myself."

"I have to do some research on robotic process automation so it might be a while, but let me know if I can get you anything."

I walked to my side of the bed, placed my glass down on the coaster on the nightstand, and situated myself comfortably on the pillows as Susan sighed deeply and turned on her side away from me.

I frowned at her being upset, but I opened my laptop and continued to do my research. I typed the letters "RPA" in a Google search box and was shown too many articles to count. I decided to tighten the search, so typed "RPA leveraging data task automation" and clicked on the first promising link. I read the article and then looped back to the information that seemed most relevant.

> **RPA can be combined with other techniques to create sophisticated data handling solutions. One example is the use of RPA to extract information from multiple clinical systems to create an appeals process for some medical necessity denials, and package those responses for a knowledge worker to review and approve, which drastically reduces human effort.**

My mind began working overtime again.

What if we can combine workflows with automation? That should help make the process more streamlined and accurate. If we can just get the right data into the correct workflow tool, and the right data back out to work with. Or maybe launching automation capabilities might do the trick. Seems practical in theory, and it should provide more power to the analytics . . .

I thought back to the conference again, that time specifically to the panel on RPA and even Doug's metrics. I must have absorbed more information that day than I had thought, including that data extraction, using RPA, is an effective poor man's interface.

So . . . what were some RPA techniques highlighted at the conference? If we take those "bots" and pair them with a real-time data driven account workflow application, that could create a meaningful solution. If only there was a way to combine these two, then the metrics Doug explained might just make sense. The only thing left to do would be to develop a more sophisticated analytic approach to monitor both the overall and detailed performance of business operations at the same time.

I tapped my fingers on the laptop before taking a drink, all the while deep in thought.

There are other tools and resources, similar to RPA, which could help remove repetitive tasks from employees: the tasks that can be easily automated, or the ones that take up the most of the employees' time. Honestly, we don't need a bigger workforce as was proposed earlier by Dave. We just need to know how the tasks can be automated to be completed more efficiently. Only then will there be a significant impact on reducing cost, increasing cash flow, and improving net revenue.

But the key question remains: what are the tools that will be useful for achieving this? I have to do some more research on RPA solutions available and the workflow solutions that can be easily integrated within JHS. I'm going to make that priority one, and priority two will be using the data to make additional analytic insights.

Satisfied and slightly excited with the discovery, I opened my email and wrote a note to remind Kim about finding the tasks that needed to be automated.

Taking one step at a time will help; because we can't eat the elephant in one big bite.

All I needed was to find a way of incorporating the two concepts within our operations and then develop a systematic implementation plan.

REVELATION

THE NEXT MORNING dawned bright and clear. The brainstorming the night before had been a good exercise.

I have a feeling we're getting close.

Having woken up earlier than usual, I decided to surprise my lovely wife with breakfast in bed. Lately, she was the one who took care of our morning caffeine fix, but today was a special day. With a smile on my face, I walked to the kitchen and began to make breakfast bowls, cracking eggs and mixing flour and milk to make sausage gravy. I started the hash browns in one pan while making sure the sausage patties were frying nicely in another.

I walked to the fridge and took out the jar of Kelly's homemade grape jam, and I popped four slices of bread into the toaster. Just as I prepared everything on a tray, the coffee machine beeped. Whistling and humming a Jason Aldean song, I picked up the tray and walked to our bedroom.

Susan was stirring. She looked at me, then at the tray in my hand, and blinked a few times.

"Is it my birthday?"

"Nope."

"Our anniversary?"

"You know that was two months ago, hon."

"Oh yeah . . . I smell coffee. Gimme."

"You haven't even washed your face yet. Ugh, how I go to bed each night with you is beyond my understanding."

She affectionately stuck out her tongue, stretched, and got up to walk to the bathroom. I placed the tray in the middle of the bed, putting the coffee mugs on the side-tables.

As I looked down at the concoction I'd created, I saw the eggs, sausage crumbles, cheese and hash browns all in the bowl, covered with sausage gravy connecting it all. I continued to stare at the collection of food, but what I started to see is how well it all came together to become breakfast. A variety of items working together for something delicious. My mind must've been in overdrive about work, because I suddenly had a vision of how we should set up our workflow solution to address the "entire universe" of accounts, so that all the seemingly disparate functions of the revenue cycle would work together to produce a highly efficient and effective process, all the while producing throughput results of a higher magnitude than we can currently . . .

"Wow, this is great! I thought you'd be hung over today," Susan joked as she joined me on the bed and sipped her coffee.

"Funny thing about last night. I went to the Trop for a beer and to think, and never got around to the actual beer."

"So, you just went to flirt with Donna?" she said with a sly grin. I chuckled and she continued. "Judging from your mood, it looks like the thinking was productive. I'm glad. You've been so stressed out these last couple weeks. I've been worried you'd get sick."

"Is that why there's a pot full of chicken noodle soup in the freezer?"

"Yes, I made it with Kelly's help."

"Wow. What did I do to deserve you?"

"I think we've had this conversation many times. And if you remember, I scored a good deal as well."

On the drive to the office, I began to think about how to introduce the concepts to the team, including my breakfast bowl revelation. I hadn't been this excited to go to work in a long time.

THE CHALLENGE

May 22

T HINKING ABOUT THE DAY BEFORE, I reviewed my earlier revelation.

If I can grab all the Aged Trial Balance detail and combine that with daily 835 remittance data along with 837 claims data, I can start to reconstruct process breakdowns. And that's only the beginning. If possible, I might be able to grab the detailed EHR audit logs to further refine the information! Once we can tell the "story" of an account, we can then construct business-rule-driven workflows and automation to improve the overall "universe" of work activity in one place and get away from "unintelligent" work queues that don't "talk" to each other.

If only I can begin to understand what the different analytics are and how to determine where exactly there's a problem that increases cost. I need to figure out how to put controls in place throughout all the processes that drive the revenue cycle, then identify those that cause net revenue loss and have been the real reason for the increasingly negative performance throughout JHS. Maybe brainstorming with the team will help come up with some ideas.

Opening the glass door of the conference room, I entered to see the four members of my team busy watching the overseas riots on TV.

How lucky have I been? My team is definitely talented, and they each bring different skills to the table. Kyle isn't tied to the historical way of doing things, so he constantly asks "why." Dave's a little older and not as much of a risk taker, but once a plan of action is agreed upon, he attacks it. Michelle is a calming presence with the mind of a "doer," and always comes through. And Kim is by far the most experienced of the four, never shy to tell me when my ideas are crazy. If ever I needed someone in a "Devil's advocate" role, this would be the time. We can't afford to get this wrong.

"Bill? Whenever you're ready." Kim nudged me out of my reflection.

I stood up and walked to the familiar whiteboard. I wrote **Mandated Goals** with the marker and underlined both words. Below that I added:

1. **8 months**
2. **Minimum of a 4% Net Revenue improvement**
2. **Minimum of a 10% reduction in Operating Expense**
4. **$20 million in Cash Flow improvement in 12 months or less**

"This is the performance improvement Terry wants from revenue cycle outcomes in the next eight months," I said. "The deadline for a solution is just about upon us. I think we've been looking at the entire problem from too much of a micro level point of view. We need to consider the throughput of the entire revenue cycle and determine where process control points break down. It's going to take all our collective abilities to achieve such a BAHG. The question is how can we get there?"

"BAHG?" Kyle asked.

Kim laughed and replied, "Big Ass Hairy Goal."

"So," I continued without cracking a smile so I wouldn't go off track, "the first thing on the table to discuss is the talent level of our revenue cycle employees.

"Recruitment comes first and foremost to my mind. While JHS has always been a large employer in this area, there have also been budget restrictions that force us to work within limitations to hire top-tier and experienced talent. Heck, with the recent expansion of Amazon into our relatively local market, even they pay more than we do. Because we operate in a tight job market, why wouldn't the good talent go to the places that can offer them more money than we do? Maybe we could pay our staff more because we need fewer of them? Think of it as a budget neutral adjustment.

"The first area of focus is talent development. I think our training approach is very limited. When was the last time we had proper monthly training sessions with new or old employees? We either have an annual training event for large groups at a time, or a 'sit with someone doing the same job' kind of training approach. This isn't an effective way to go about developing superior talent."

"I agree," Dave said, "but we simply don't have the time to put together specific individual training programs. We also don't have enough information to know what each person needs. We've talked about this already." Dave's pragmatism, while frustrating at times, was usually spot on.

"The point I'm trying to make," I continued, "is that we're still using the same old processes and approaches we've used for the last twenty years. Sure, some advances have been made, but we still do things with the same mentality we've always had. We've failed to adapt to the changes of the industry overall. Our thinking has to change if we want to survive. Making sure the current employees are giving their very best is also an important factor, so the sheer size of our team should also be considered. With roughly 650 FTEs, it's almost impossible to know how everyone is performing in the current environment. And on top of that, there are some managers and supervisors who let things slide with their favorite employees."

"So how do you propose we fix it?" Kim asked, direct and to the point.

"The simplest approach is to shift our thinking to understand things like account throughput and functional specific outcomes. With that, I'm hopeful we can identify which employees are effective and which ones are not, thus opening the door for individualized training."

In a measured tone, Dave said, "Well, from what my people tell me, if we didn't have so many errors from Patient Access, cash flow would be a lot healthier."

Kyle immediately flushed and barked out, "That's right, everything is always our fault. I guess it doesn't matter that we get the wrong information from our managed care department on what services need prior authorization or anything like that, huh? I ask you all the time to provide detailed information on what you see so I can try to fix the problems, but all I get are a handful of screen prints and accusations."

"Whoa, calm down, guys. No one's accusing anybody here."

"Bill's right," Kim said. "Look guys, there's enough blame to go around. But we should focus on fixing our individual problems before pointing fingers, right? Don't tell me you've forgotten Rule 5 already. 'Complaining isn't an action step.'"

This elicited chuckles from the group, and the tension eased. It looked like I wouldn't have to intervene and play referee after all.

"When I was sitting in a bar the other night waiting for my drink," I continued, "my mind went to the earlier days of my career. Has it ever occurred to any of you that with all the changes to our industry that have come from technology—electronic health record advances, administrative simplification, and reimbursement mechanisms—we're still basically doing the work the same way we've always done it? Sure, we have things like web portals instead of phone calls, but the results haven't changed significantly. Even performance measurement has remained the same. I think the problem is that we don't have the metrics that provide the insights to make dramatic changes and improvements.

"And then yesterday, when I was eating breakfast—which included a bunch of things that I put together in one bowl, and which I might add was pretty awesome . . ." More chuckles. "It occurred to me that everything in the bowl—eggs, sausage, hash browns, gravy—was working together better than any individual ingredient. I began to piece together the combination of advanced workflow, RPA, and augmented analytics as a cohesive approach to our problems."

Kim replied, "But as you've taught us to always ask, 'So what? Is it important?'"

"Humor me for a minute. What if the time-tested performance measures are no longer valid, or at least not of primary significance? What if instead of helping us understand performance and identify issues, they're actually hindering us from making significant gains related to revenue cycle outcomes?"

A beat of silence passed, but then Dave pointed out the obvious. "Boss, I'm more than willing to listen, but every healthcare provider in the country uses some form of these metrics. They can't all be wrong."

"Well, Dave, everyone used to use a horse and buggy until the car was invented," Kyle replied, probably still a little salty about Dave's earlier comments.

"Kyle, that's different," Dave rapidly responded back. The back-and-forth between the two reminded me once again how different their two personalities are, as Kyle would jump right into something new while Dave would want to think about it, taking his time. This is one reason I had hired both men, because I knew the constant back-and-forth would yield results if directed in the right way.

"No, actually Kyle is correct," I said. "What if this is a new way to look at revenue cycle operations and see what no one else has seen? We're under the gun to make material improvements in what would appear to be an aggressive timeframe, and I firmly believe that after studying our management packs of standard reports, we have to find a new way forward."

A knock sounded on the door, then Shannon walked in and said, "Excuse me, Bill, but Rebecca called and would like you to run down to her office. She said it was urgent."

With a deep sigh I turned to Kim and told her, "Please keep this moving forward. Hopefully, I won't be gone long."

What could Rebecca want that would possibly be this urgent?

SURPRISE HELP

May 25

ALL MY FRUSTRATIONS were clearly showing by the time I reached Rebecca's office, as I plopped into a chair and unceremoniously said, "Well, I'm here. What did you want to talk about?"

"Hello to you too, Bill."

"Sorry, my mind's somewhere else."

"Tell me about it. You've been running your team haggard these past several days."

Both of us laughed, and Rebecca stood up from her chair and walked to my side of the desk, leaning back against it. "Look, Bill, I can't really put it more clearly than this. If you don't find a solution soon, we all fail. It's no longer a question of whether you lose your job, but whether we all do. In fact, the one good thing from all this is that it made it a little easier to get this authorized."

She picked up a sheet of paper from the desk and handed to me. It was a printout of an email exchange between her and Terry, showing his approval for extra budget to the revenue cycle department.

"Oh, this is wonderful. Thank you!"

"I told him this is the only way we can help you and your department pull off the turnaround. However . . ."

"Ah, there it is."

"However, Terry only agreed to give the budget increase as a loan, which means you *have* to hit or increase stated net revenue improvements, or the difference will be made up by eliminating members of your team. I'm sorry, but it's the best I could get out of him at this point."

"No, no, I completely understand. Rebecca, you've already done too much. Again, thank you . . . and I won't disappoint."

"First things first. You know Terry is a very metrics-driven executive. You'll need to develop standardized analytics to track improvement progress tied to these changes. I'm worried that our current IT department can't handle the level of analytics required, so let me recommend that the first thing you do is hire a data analyst and develop an analysis platform. I've already talked to Steve, the head of IT, to set up a special Tableau Software server environment that will be dedicated to your efforts.

"Also, I'd like you to consider my niece, Marie Simpson, as a candidate for the analyst role. You don't need to hire her based on my recommendation, but evaluate her like you would anyone else. She's fresh out of college and is eager to start a career in healthcare. Her background is in analytics, which is why I recommend her."

"Of course. Just email me her resume. Is that it?"

"Yes, Bill. And take a deep breath."

I laughed again. "Really, thank you. I needed this kind of news."

"Well, you work hard, Bill, and I want to help as much as I can. You just take care of the results."

With a nod, I stood up and walked towards the door with a smile on my face that wasn't there when I had entered. I was feeling fresher and more energized than I had for days.

THROUGHPUT

May 26

"So, TERRY AGREED to give us a 'loan?' At least they haven't lost total faith in us." It was pizza and pasta day at the JHS cafeteria, and Kim and I were getting in a quick lunch. "And Rebecca wants you to hire her niece? That's some pretty bald-faced nepotism right there."

"She only said to look into her profile. But Rebecca wouldn't have recommended her if she didn't trust her."

"Great, then hire her and let's be done with it. We have so much to do, we can't mess around and waste time searching for the perfect candidate. What about workflow automation solutions?"

"Well, there are only a few healthcare-focused solutions available in the market. I've narrowed down to three companies at this point."

"This is why I tell Chris it would be hard to be in your job. I'm not sure I'm capable of all you do."

"Ah, most days it's a good life . . . although yes, I'd like to be seeing my wife more often than I am right now."

Later in my office, I pulled up the website of one of the automation company finalists and read through it in more detail so I could fully understand the nuances of advanced workflow as compared to our current work queue capabilities.

Workflow automation makes complicated business processes easier to manage. When a task is completed, automated workflows can move or transform data according to business-driven rules. By leveraging sophisticated workflow automation, human variability is vastly removed, allowing for significant productivity gains and improved financial outcomes. Work is only presented to a Knowledge Worker when the automation hits an exception, such as denial of payment by insurance companies. The end result of the standardization and automation of workflow for healthcare organizations is significant annual net revenue improvements and reduced FTE costs.

While clearer in my understanding, I was still no closer to making a decision among the three companies. Suddenly a name popped up in my mind. Who's the perfect person to ask for a second opinion, but Doug? Since our initial interactions, I had been in touch with Doug fairly regularly.

I shot him an email, and a bit later received his reply:

Remember our last conversation? You need to think about the "next most valuable" concept. Whatever the solution or software is, you will have to use it with some regularity to figure out its value for your process. In the end, the workflow IS really important, there are no exceptions to this, but getting a high degree of automation is what you really need more than anything.

The next day, the team was back in my office, and we resumed our work.

"So as a reminder, throughput is a measure of how many units of work a system can process in a given amount of time," I said, once we were underway. "It's applied broadly to workflow concepts, from various aspects of computer and network systems to organizations. Related measures of system productivity include the speed with which some specific workload can be completed and the response time—the amount of time between a single interactive user request and receipt of the response."

"So basically," Kim asked, "if one part of a process isn't efficient, the entire process isn't?"

"Right. I want to improve the throughput of the entire revenue cycle department and not just one area. So that means the work performance of each individual part must contribute to overall throughput of the entire ecosystem. What are the areas you feel we need to improve that others are waiting on?" I wrote **IMPROVEMENTS** on the whiteboard.

Michelle said, "Medical records? I'm beginning to see why it would be one of the key areas that could impact OER."

"Exactly." I wrote it on the board.

Kyle piped in. "Well, I think we can possibly improve one part of the process by reducing the volume of rejected claims—prebilling holds for coding, claim clearinghouse holds, payer first-pass rejections, things like that."

The talk then moved to the concept of the operational efficiency ratio and enhancing FTE performance. I glanced at Dave, who had a determined glint in his eye and his "thinking hard" expression on his face. Before long he said, "Okay, stop me if I'm rambling, but what if we eliminate a lot of the redundant manual activities that follow-up staff have to perform? A lot of time is spent on tasks like checking on a claim status, so if we automate just that alone, the throughput would surely increase. I'm not talking about basic electronic data interchange through our clearinghouse, but true detailed responses that typically only a human receives."

"Essentially, we would be impacting both the effectiveness and efficiency ratios," Kyle responded.

"That's right."

"Could possibly work . . ."

The next few minutes were spent discussing the McPherson Principle, process throughput, and how all of the concepts could be applied in one work prioritization and automation solution. A lot was accomplished today. I decided to call it a win.

▲▼▲

My last task of the day was to message Doug.

I have a proposition to make. I'd like to invite you to come onsite to meet the team and hear about our progress. I think you'll be able to provide valuable insight, considering you've been offering consultation to us for a while now. I look forward to hearing what you think.

THE VISIT

June 2

A WEEK LATER, Doug was in the conference room, explaining the concept of "next most valuable" to my team in more detail.

"So, business rules, not employee preference, should drive work and task prioritization, and that routing should be sent to staff groups that do very similar activities, if possible, to be able to compare staff and process outcomes. This allows management to focus on individual micro-performance improvement, which will then drive overall improvements. This is how business performance and outcomes can be changed for the better."

"Where does robotic automation come into the picture?"

"Excellent question, Dave. Consider that before computers, or even calculators, people still did math with just pen and paper. The invention of calculators made lives easier. RPA is similar; it's just a fancy new term for some old school automation techniques, but with more artificial intelligence."

Then Terry popped his head into the room. "Ah, here they are," he said, walking over and shaking Doug's hand. "It's nice to meet you, Doug. I looked into your background and was very impressed. Bill was lucky to have crossed paths with you."

"I've had some interesting conversations with Bill," Doug responded. "I think he's on the way to creating some very innovative solutions that will improve outcomes dramatically around here. We were just discussing his idea to prioritize work by the concept of value."

Terry seemed surprised . . . and dare I say, a little impressed? "Well, I'll leave you to it," he said, heading out. "Bill, don't forget, Doug's fees will have to be part of your improvement outcomes."

I nodded and he left. The entire room collectively exhaled. "Thanks for sticking up for us," I said to Doug.

He smiled. "No problem. I'm a consultant, so I'm used to sticky situations."

"More like a walk through an active minefield," Kim said, which got a hearty laugh from us all.

▲▼▲

"Kim, I love these 'Hot and Now' doughnuts from Krispy Kreme. They're so good. And fresh!"

I had rented an offsite meeting room so the regular team and Doug would have undisturbed privacy during the planning phase. It was Saturday, and we were getting into it again. Kyle was already on his third doughnut.

"This is a big moment for all of us," Doug was saying, "and we need to make sure that the rest of the revenue cycle team fully understands not only the magnitude of the work to be accomplished, but the change in thinking and acting that must occur to be ultimately successful. We're talking massive change when it comes to how people think about their jobs, how they perform their jobs, and how they're rewarded for their jobs. To be blunt about it, that change in mindset has to start with the five of you or it won't ever seep down to your staff.

"Now, from what I've seen so far, you're more than willing to take on the challenge, but willingness won't be enough. You'll need discipline and patience as well, in order to ensure you stay true to the new way of valuing work, and that you're helping your staff through the journey. Remember, this isn't just about ratios and concepts—those are just a means to an end. The real value is driving significant and sustainable results. Currently, JHS is a highly reactive environment. When a patient is scheduled for a visit, we react by checking to verify their insurance, and react again by obtaining authorization. After service is performed, we react by trying to determine the appropriate billing codes to put on a claim. After we bill that claim, we react with a follow-up when a claim isn't paid and try to retroactively determine root cause issues for avoidable write-offs. Nothing you do is really proactive, and that needs to change.

"We need to develop a plan that is proactive through the use of RPA with patient access, health information management, and patient financial services activities. Proactive with early automatic determination of claim status, so that you can resolve issues before a payer notifies you of non-payment. Proactive with forcing payers to process claims at a faster pace. Proactive in how you deal with your staff and their performance. Before we get into the specifics of the plan design, does anyone have any questions?"

Never shy, Kyle responded, "I'm excited about all this, but how are we supposed to learn and implement these major changes while still doing our day jobs?"

"I'll be bringing in my own external team to help with the implementation and project management. As far as training the leadership team on new concepts, that's one of my primary roles on the project." Doug concluded.

"Guys," I said, "we have all the data in front of us concerning other companies who have tried and succeeded using similar variations of these solutions, both within and outside the healthcare industry. All we need to do is come up with a performance improvement plan that encompasses them. Let's walk through them one more time. First, the operational efficiency ratio." I wrote on the whiteboard:

$$OER = \frac{\# \text{ new DNFB}}{\# \text{ released DNFB}} + \frac{\# \text{ new A/R}}{\# \text{ resolved A/R}}$$

"To remind you, this ratio should be less than two. If it's more, the inflows are greater than the outflows, and backlogs will form as a result. Overall, cash will decrease related to the collection of accounts—which is very similar to some of our current operational performance," I said with a somber tone that matched my mood. While we seemed to have mad real progress, I was feeling the pressure to make actual improvements.

Dave then stood and asked, "Mind if I take a run at explaining the others? I just want to make sure I'm understanding them correctly."

"Feel free." I handed him the marker.

"The process effectiveness ratio formula goes like this . . ."

$$PER = First\ Pass\ Rejection\ Volume\ /\ Total\ Claims$$

"This ratio should be less than 2 percent. If it's greater then significant process breakdowns exist, and they'll have a material impact on FTE costs to rework errors. If it's less than 2 percent, there should be a direct impact on operating cost reduction, increased throughput, and cash flow improvement."

Doug went on to say, "Improving operational effectiveness is critical to this initiative. Business rule driven work prioritization across revenue cycle operations will help mitigate payer denial activities, which will improve throughput and improve bottom line performance."

"And that gets us to the employee performance ratio," Dave said. "Let's see if I get this right . . ."

Step 1:   *(# of Resolution Actions) + (# of Processing Actions × .25) = Effectiveness Score*

Step 2:   *(Effectiveness Score / Performance Base) × 100 = Employee Performance Ratio*

"As we've documented," he continued, "the various performance base measurements are as follows:"

1. Preregistration: 40
2. Coding:
   a. Inpatient: 20
   b. Observation: 14
   c. Ambulatory Surgery: 30
   d. Outpatient: 155
   e. Emergency Room: 175
3. Billing: 140
4. Third Party Follow-up: 50

"It's used as a way to analytically understand how much an FTE contributes to successful and positive completion of work activities. In its simplest form, this is the volume and quality of work performed combined into one metric, but it goes much deeper than that in reality."

Kyle looked over the room, then asked, "From a tactical perspective, Dave, how do we track user actions to know if they're a resolution or not? We don't have that information."

"Good point," echoed Dave. "We have a hard enough time just requesting useful productivity numbers."

"The features and functionality of the workflow solution will help in that regard," Doug clarified.

"And to remind you," I said very matter-of-factly, "the results of the improvement plan must be shown in eight months, with a minimum of 4 percent improvement in net revenue, a minimum of a 10 percent reduction in operating expense, and $20 million in cash flow improvement in twelve months or less.

"From our discussion, it seems clear that we need a rules-driven workflow solution instead of our current work queue capabilities, coupled with RPA tools to drive a high degree of automation, if we plan to drive dramatic gains in operational performance. Then we need to supplement the work with augmented analytics, so that as a management team we can monitor the new ratios and ensure results are achieved. Does everyone agree?"

Everyone in the room nodded.

"Doug, anything we missed?" I asked.

"No, I think you covered it."

"Where's the list of workflow prioritization system options?"

Dave flipped open the Moleskine notebook he carried everywhere. "Here it is, Bill. Our shortlist includes AccountStream, ProWorkflow, and Vispa."

"Doug, you have more experience with system selections than we do. Any suggestions?"

"Personally, I would compare the three options on the following criteria at a minimum." He grabbed a dry erase marker, moved to the whiteboard, and wrote:

1) **Speed of implementation**
2) **Ability to support implementation with data support services**
3) **Flexibility of business rules configuration**
4) **Ability to support the "next most valuable" routing concept**
5) **Automation support capabilities**

After a half-hour of discussion and a weighted vote, the clear winner was Vispa.

"Let's talk deployment next. Doug and I think it would be best to implement in patient financial services first, to start to drive improved cash flow through expedited account resolution, and then we'll work in patient access and concurrently address medical records as soon as Dave's area is complete."

"Great. You know we're up for the challenge," Kyle said enthusiastically.

"Simultaneously, we'll roll out our augmented analytics using Tableau Software," I continued. "That will allow us to track all revenue cycle functional areas, including patient access, revenue assurance, and patient financial services. We'll also implement the tracking of the three ratios we discussed, and the analytic framework will utilize natural language processing as well. Work on advanced employee productivity and effectiveness tracking in real time will also be implemented. The plan will consist of a four-month rollout, including developing the appropriate data model and ingestion into both workflow and analytics, development of automation, staff training on job function performance and technical training on new tools, and management training on new performance expectations as well.

"In conjunction with installing Vispa and Tableau Software, we'll also incorporate various RPA bots where appropriate. In order to ensure that these changes maximize return, I'll also conduct quarterly reviews to ensure that continuous improvement is achieved." I paused and let out a long breath. "And then hopefully we all finally get a good night's sleep."

THE PRESENTATION

June 9—Seven Months until the Deadline

AFTER WEEKS OF WORK, we had finally come up with a good plan, one that could be successful if executed well. The morning of the big presentation to the Board, I dressed in my favorite gray suit and lucky blue tie, which I'd dubbed "lucky" since I'd had it on at a conference when I won a trip to Mexico. Before leaving for work, I went to the kitchen to grab a quick toast and tea and laughed when I saw that Susan had prepared a full continental breakfast. "You made such a huge spread!" I exclaimed.

"I think I'm more nervous than you are."

"What's to be nervous about? Just because I'll be fired if this doesn't go well?"

She frowned. "They wouldn't really let you go, would they?"

I shrugged. "There's no reason to worry. I've been in touch with a few recruiters. Just in case." I made a few selections from the awesome breakfast bar and tucked them in a bag.

"Well, I have a lot of faith in my husband." She gave me a kiss. "Now go be fabulous."

Upon arrival to the hospital, I walked straight to the boardroom without stopping by my office. After fifteen minutes of tinkering with my laptop and the projector, I sat down and waited for the Board members to arrive, which they started doing one by one.

"These Board meetings seem to get earlier and earlier," said veteran member Elijah upon entering. "I'm too old to be up this early in the day."

"Don't mind him," said Sharon, a local banker. "He hasn't had coffee yet." She gave me a warm smile.

"Well, then let me treat," I said enthusiastically. "Um, no sugar in yours, right, Sharon?"

"That's right. Nice of you to remember, Bill." Yes, I got my 50/50 blind guess correct! I'm playing with house money today!

The next few minutes were spent on small talk, until everyone started making their way to their respective seats. Terry snuck in right as the clock announced the start time, the usual look of irritation on his face. He seemed to make it a point to always be the last person to enter a room.

"When you're ready." Rebecca, sitting across from him, gave me an encouraging smile.

This is it. The moment of truth. I took a deep breath and walked to the television screen. The laptop was open and ready. Everyone's attention was on me.

"As you all know, I've been tasked to come up with a revenue cycle performance improvement plan, and for the past few months my team and I have been working diligently to develop a path to improvement for revenue cycle operations. We've discovered some interesting theories about why performance has dropped considerably at JHS over the past eighteen months, and the data collected from our research has yielded highly specific info on the subject.

"Using detailed payer remittance data, we evaluated first pass rejections and grouped them into categories, based on the most likely process area that would have caused the breakdown. As you can see in the following chart, we've identified eight categories of payment rejection activity and the associated volume and dollar amount." A click of the wireless controller button brought a bigger image of a graph titled, *Overall First Pass Rejection Analysis.*

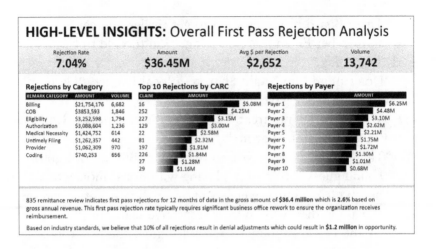

HIGH-LEVEL INSIGHTS: Overall First Pass Rejection Analysis

Rejection Rate	Amount	Avg $ per Rejection	Volume
7.04%	$36.45M	$2,652	13,742

Rejections by Category

REMARK CATEGORY	AMOUNT	VOLUME
Billing	$21,754,176	6,682
COB	$3853,593	1,846
Eligibility	$3,252,598	1,794
Authorization	$3,088,604	1,236
Medical Necessity	$1,424,752	614
Untimely Filing	$1,262,357	442
Provider	$1,062,309	970
Coding	$740,253	656

Top 10 Rejections by CARC

CLAIM	AMOUNT
16	$5.08M
252	$4.25M
227	$3.15M
129	$3.00M
22	$2.58M
81	$2.32M
197	$1.91M
226	$1.84M
27	$1.28M
29	$1.16M

Rejections by Payer

	AMOUNT
Payer 1	$6.25M
Payer 2	$4.48M
Payer 3	$3.10M
Payer 4	$2.62M
Payer 5	$2.21M
Payer 6	$1.75M
Payer 7	$1.72M
Payer 8	$1.30M
Payer 9	$1.01M
Payer 10	$0.68M

835 remittance review indicates first pass rejections for 12 months of data in the gross amount of **$36.4 million** which is **2.6%** based on gross annual revenue. This first pass rejection rate typically requires significant business office rework to ensure the organization receives reimbursement.

Based on industry standards, we believe that 10% of all rejections result in denial adjustments which could result in **$1.2 million** in opportunity.

"As you can see, we were able to isolate the increased claim volume for follow-up activities due to ever-growing rejections, and we learned that we lack the benefit of utilizing automation tools to reduce the overall volume of work that our staff needs to get through. An increase in prebilling holds has been impacting overall throughput, and we determined that we need to review the detailed claim translation data on a regular basis, which will allow us to automatically correct repetitive claim errors. We also learned that an increase in front-end process and data quality errors has been requiring rework by our already overwhelmed back-end staff. And finally, the data made us realize that high-volume manual tasks are taking too much time away from our staff's ability to perform critical functions.

"These process breakdowns impact financial outcomes and are further exacerbated by the technology and systems JHS has been using to manage these functions. The plan that my team and I created primarily focuses on technical enablers. We came up with the following solutions."

Another click brought up the next slide. I felt myself relax a little. Just a little.

"After careful consideration," I continued, "we've decided to implement the Vispa workflow prioritization solution. This will allow us to improve automation, reduce FTE workloads, and monitor staff productivity and effectiveness. The duration for this is six to eight weeks. The second step is the use of advanced augmented analytics to implement the first module, patient financial services, which will last four weeks. Then comes process automation and advanced reporting, which is planned for eight weeks.

"During this period our teams, along with an external consulting group, will identify those high-volume activities that can be automated, and the Vispa team will develop bots for our use. After that we'll tackle the revenue assurance process redesign and staff training, which we estimate will take twelve weeks. Patient access process redesign and staff training will come last, and will be given roughly six to eight weeks for us to complete. In all, it should result in a one-time cash flow of $24 million, annual net revenue improvements of $52 million, and annual cost reduction of $1.2 million. We should be able to achieve the mandated results at a minimum.

"I realize this is a lot of information, so I'll pause here for questions." My request was met with silence.

Gulp. Given the lackluster response to my plan at the previous Board meeting where I was essentially laughed out of the room, I felt a moment of trepidation.

Finally, Jim Murphy spoke. "I have to say, based on the last time we met, I didn't expect such a well-thought-out plan. The overall analysis seems very thorough and comprehensive. Terry?"

Terry continued staring at the screen a moment, then turned to me. "I'll be honest with you, Bill. Until today, I wasn't sure that you were the right person for this monumental task. But honestly, you've managed to impress me."

I exhaled a breath I didn't realize I'd been holding.

The next few minutes were spent answering various questions about details, but all the Board members seemed content, and the meeting ended with their unanimous approval to move forward.

As the meeting broke up, Terry came over and put a hand on my shoulder. "Great job. I mean that sincerely." He let go and started walking away. "Now, let's see this through."

Wow, Terry actually gave me a compliment. Wait till I tell Kim. She won't believe it.

I looked at the wall clock and was surprised to see that it was already late morning. *The meeting had taken that long?* I decided to take the rest of the day off. The past several weeks had been so stressful, and I had earned a few hours to decompress. On the way to my car, my thoughts went to Susan.

She deserves something nice too, since this win wouldn't have been possible without her support and encouragement. I think I'll pick up roses and a bottle of wine, put the kids to bed early tonight, and my wife and I can celebrate.

WORK PRIORITIZATION

June 8

"CAN WE GO OVER 'next most valuable' one more time for our account processing?"

It was day two of the Vispa implementation. Kyle, Doug, Dave, Michelle, and two members of Doug's team, John and Cassie, were sitting around the round conference table, looking at me.

"Sure, Kyle. It basically means that the next highest valued account—however we want to define it—that requires human interaction is queued to a worker for action, depending on the job function and business rules. Ideally, we want to only present an account to a representative as it needs to be worked and in the order that management deems will have the most valuable impact."

John chimed in. "Determining the next move valuable for the staff to work is a bit tricky, but the Vispa system is highly configurable."

Kyle furrowed his brow. "Hmm. So how do accounts interact with each other?"

Doug jumped back into the conversation. "The Vispa team will map your payer master file in your core system to an internal payer master in Vispa, and then every day new account updates are imported into the system. An automated bot will deploy and check the claim status for all payers and post the information it captures to what they call the 'timeline' in Vispa. This will help each user who accesses that account know what needs to be accomplished to resolve it."

Dave rubbed his chin for a moment, deep in thought, and then said, "Then that should eliminate a rep from getting an account they don't need to address? For example, when a payer portal tells us that a claim is set to pay on a certain date?"

"Yes," Doug replied. "Our initial testing with your payer master last week indicates that the system will reduce the accounts touched by 25 to 30 percent."

"Wow!" Kyle exclaimed.

"Wait until you see the testing results for the Patient Access automation," Doug added with a grin.

"Okay, guys," I said to reel them back in to the task at hand. "The Vispa team has already begun working on the import routine for the daily aged trial balance (ATB), the 837 claim forms—both hospital and physician—the 835 payer remittance data, and all the posted payments and adjustments. This will allow the rep to have all the information needed to help them work the account in an efficient and effective manner. No more flipping through multiple screens."

"Right, Bill," Doug said. "What we need to do next is review the actions in the Vispa application that track what a rep does to the account and determine whether it's a 'resolution' action that moves it along to the next step for adjudication, or a 'processing' action that doesn't. We'll use these to monitor employee performance and develop micro-training."

Then Doug looked over at Cassie, who began projecting Vispa configuration pages to the large television in the room. "I'm currently displaying the 'actions' a user can take to demonstrate what they physically did to the account, so we can monitor them in detail," she said. "Let's go over each one to ensure they're routing correctly, and to determine if we need to add additional action codes." With that, the team got started.

▲▼▲

Later, I was sitting in my office, my mind wandering. Doug knocked on the doorframe and leaned in. "Have a second?"

"Of course," I said, because I didn't really have a choice. "I'm just reviewing the training plan Cassie emailed me earlier." I smiled.

"You know," Doug responded with a smirk, "sometimes you're a terrible liar." I couldn't help but chuckle. He and I were becoming friends, which made the time together go that much faster. And no doubt more productive.

Doug dropped into a guest chair. "That training plan is exactly what I wanted to talk to you about. When we kick off the employee sessions in a few weeks, my team and the Vispa team will handle most of the actual training, but I think it'll be important for you to open the sessions with positive comments about what JHS is trying to accomplish and why, and speak positively about the new solutions, especially Vispa and the 'next most valuable' concept. It's one thing hearing it from consultants, but your employees will get behind things a lot more if they know you believe in the approach. Change scares people."

I chuckled. "Yeah, I know. I will absolutely express my enthusiasm, as well as my concerns if they don't embrace the changes." As I said the last bit, I couldn't help but reflect on how much pushback I'd be getting from the staff.

▲▼▲

As I got in my car to leave that evening, I looked down at my watch and felt a slight bit of shock at the fact that it was already eight o'clock. *Good thing Susan is out with some of her neighborhood friends for Women's Wine Night.*

I eventually put the kids to bed, and as I was making a grilled cheese sandwich, I heard the doorknob fumbling. My beautiful wife entered the kitchen, stumbled a little, and smiled as she looked at me. "Hey there, handsome man," she managed to say without too much trouble.

"Well, hello there, sexy lady," I replied, flipping my grilled cheese in the pan. She came over and whispered in my ear. I paused for a quick moment, then turned off the stove and took her hand, leaving the half-finished grilled cheese in its pan. The damn sandwich could wait!

AUTOMATION

July 24

HAVING HAD A MUCH BETTER EVENING than I'd planned, I showed up to work in a great mood the next day. Grabbing a hot cup of coffee from the stand in the lobby, I headed straight to the conference room near my office that we'd converted into a busy command center.

As I passed by my office door, my assistant, Shannon, said, "Boss, Rebecca wants to see you. And no, I don't have a clue what she wants."

Truthfully, Shannon is the best assistant anyone would ever want. She works late, never complains, and just gets stuff done. If I ever lost her, I'd be crushed . . . and most likely highly ineffective for weeks.

I decided to check in with my team before looking for Rebecca.

The conversation was in full gear when I walked into the command center. "It is, but Kyle and I will work on this in tandem . . ." Dave was saying as I strolled in. "One of the things we've discussed are the front-end errors in Patient Access. We have to map out the eligibility process and use Vispa and RPA to automate as much as possible."

Dave paused as he noticed me, but I nodded for him to continue. "Currently we grab all the patient insurance and demographics information at the time of appointment scheduling—for those who schedule—and the rest we pick up when they show up at a facility to register or are a direct admit from the emergency room. In all three situations, we manually kick off the eligibility and verification process. Even though the system automatically checks against our clearinghouse, we still need to 'click the button' to initiate the process. Also, we typically only check high dollar cases due to staffing limitations. This allows for human error and missed accounts, even though we try to do it several days in advance."

"That's correct about missing some transactions and human error," Doug replied. "But as our preliminary automation testing has shown, by implementing the process on Vispa, the tasks are more much more efficient and have a higher degree of accuracy." He gave me a sideways glance, implying that I should add my two cents and hopefully break up whatever tension the team was feeling.

"I thought long and hard on my way in to work today," I started, looking at everyone around the table with a serious frown. "And what I concluded is we should definitely order in lunch from the Tropicana!"

Smiles spread around the room, so I continued. "Dave, let's give the workflow and automation a shot. You keep mentioning that eligibility payer rejections are such a time waster when it comes to follow-up. If what Doug says holds true, we'll reduce that volume by over 80 percent." The attitude in the room slowly moved back more to a discussion about problem solving.

"All right . . ." Doug said as the meeting finally neared an end. "So the rest of the week should be spent working out the kinks of patient access and eligibility with the RPA programmer on the Vispa team. John from my team, working with Kyle, will put together an update by this Friday and bring the results back to the team. Kyle, as discussed, we'll need you to develop a detailed report of the RPA modifications needed to make the processing more precise, and the results of this additional detailed testing will allow us to quickly deal with any issues that arise."

"Works for me," Kyle said. "I do have one question though, boss." I nodded at him to continue. "Will you order me the chicken quesadilla?"

That brought a few light chuckles around the room as we packed up.

After stopping by my office to drop things off, I headed to Rebecca's. Once there, I saw the door was ajar, so I peeked in and knocked on the doorframe. "Good morning. Or afternoon. Whatever it is now. I heard you wanted to see me?"

"I did," she said flatly, not looking up from her computer monitor. "I've been going over your last month's P&L. Looks like we're burning through some high amounts in both consulting fees and overtime pay." Now she looked up and I could see her displeasure.

"Terry said that as long as I cover my costs in additional improvement, I had an open budget," I replied defensively.

"Bill, be realistic. You don't have an open budget. He said that he'd support additional spending, but there has to be some realism to it. What's your progress? Are we making any headway? So far, I don't see any material change in performance outcomes." She walked over to her espresso machine and started to make a cup.

"You've been supportive of my approach until now. What's changed?"

"Well, who do you think has to explain the expense increase to the Board? I'm constantly having to defend you these days, and it gets a little stressful." Her latte ready, she took a long drink and sighed. "I'm sorry for being a little combative. I had a rough finance committee meeting last night. Until the improvements come through, our cash position isn't very strong, and I'm beginning to worry about potentially tripping our bond covenants if we're not careful." I looked at my normally unflappable boss with a fresh lens.

"Look," I said, "we're making incredible progress right now. It should translate into improved financial outcomes soon."

"Will, Bill, will."

"Excuse me?"

"You're making progress that *will* translate into improved financial outcomes soon. Saying they *should* improve isn't comforting."

"Ah, I see. I *will* ensure that we produce positive results. I can already see some progress. Poor word choice on my part." I smiled to show my confidence.

"Just please try to give me a heads-up in the future if you think your spend will be high in any major category. That'll give me time to put together an effective defensive position." She returned to her desk, sat down, and looked up at me. "Now, go out there and make me some money."

△▽△

Later that day, the team was back in the conference room. "The way I see it," I was saying, "implementation of the software is just one step out of many. We also need to retrain the team and see how they handle the new changes. Not everyone will be able to, especially if they've gotten adept at doing all the tasks manually. I suspect the reps who've been around a while will take more time to teach than our newer staff members, but it could be the other way around. Also, Kyle, Dave, and Michelle, you three will have to adjust how you review and manage performance. That might take a bit of time as well."

"Are you saying we're a bunch of old dogs who can't learn new tricks?" Dave asked with a smile.

Kyle piled on. "Come on, boss. We all know Dave is slow, but at least I'm going to pick up this stuff quickly." Seeing the team joking during a highly stressful time was heartening, and I said a quick thank you one more time for their commitment.

"All right, all right, let's get back to it," Kim said. "Next up is our prior authorization for treatment problem. This problem has been increasing industry-wide, as insurance companies continue to aggressively update their provider policies and work to control the cost side of their financial position. Authorization obtainment has become a pivotal issue and several providers in the industry are exploring ways to automate the process, or at least to use advanced workflow to control the obtainment activity."

Doug picked things up. "We need to deploy Vispa in a way that first determines if a patient is eligible for the required clinical service. Different insurance companies have different eligibility standards and limits, so there's a lot of back and forth just to check. Only after that can we obtain the authorization to proceed."

"The managed care department had already sent us lists of the policies of the top insurance companies for authorization obtainment," Kyle said. "We then supplemented that list with the last twelve months of payer rejections for lack of authorization. After developing this full list, we built those checks into Vispa, to either obtain authorization through the use of RPA bots or manually push the activity to a patient access knowledge worker if the automation failed for any reason.

"Our initial testing showed an 87 percent rate of completion for eligibility confirmation and a 41 percent rate of authorization obtainment. We need to fine-tune the bots somewhat, but these results are very exciting. Performing these tasks manually took a lot of time; and although it's just been one week of implementation, the improvement in efficiency has been dramatic. In addition, we'll be eliminating human error in the process, which should impact the reps' work on the back end to expedite payment. Boss, I think this is just the beginning. The more we learn what RPA and Vispa can do together, the more improvements I think we can make!"

"So what's next on the docket to resolve?" I asked to keep the team moving.

"The follow-up of accounts that get denied," Dave said. "This is where the reps' process begins. After implementing automation related to advanced claim status, we were able to reduce the outstanding number of open accounts needing human intervention by more than 25 percent and reduce the manual work on the phone and web portal that my team usually has to do. The account processing has been expedited, and the same tasks that used to take so much time are now being done more quickly and efficiently.

"By implementing Vispa, we now have all the necessary information in a concise fashion under one platform, as well as all the demographics' information of anything related to the status of an account. As a result, account processing is quicker and more accurate, and the effectiveness is much cleaner." Dave was as excited as Kyle, and Dave never gets excited.

"Awesome," I said enthusiastically. "I never thought we'd see such drastic improvements in such a short time!"

"What about employee productivity and effectiveness?" Kim asked. "When we do need a knowledge worker to intervene? This is one of the main reasons we implemented these tools in the first place."

"That's the best part," Kyle replied. "We no longer have a staffing problem, because automation has taken away the need to justify additional FTEs. Costs are mitigated without having to hire more employees."

"What do we have to focus on next to keep up the pace?" I asked, wanting to pour gas on this fire that had excited everyone.

"I'll jump in here," Doug said. "Now that we're beginning to track employee performance, we need to develop what we call 'micro education' plans, which essentially means developing training for each individual based on their unique needs. My team will conduct these with your managers for a few weeks and then transition to your team for the long-term. The training will focus on action steps that will help improve productivity and effectiveness of individuals, which, in turn, will bring a dramatic improvement to the team as a whole. Let me convene with my team, and by next week we'll have the initial individual plans completed."

"Sounds like a plan. Good progress, everyone. I'm definitely pleased." I couldn't help but smile as I finished the statement.

THE METRICS

August 10

As we worked through the fine-tuning of the Vispa and RPA implementation and a few weeks of conducting employee micro training, we figured it was time to really start leveraging our analytic tools, utilizing Tableau Software as our base application. We decided to move forward with a Tableau extension for Natural Language Generation, using a tool called Automated Insights from the company Wordsmith. Through these combined analytic solutions, we hoped to easily monitor all components of revenue cycle operations, including specific employee performance monitoring. This meant that a new person was now joining us for our daily team meetings, Tableau specialist Marie Simpson.

"I think the first thing we should do is address the elephant in the room," Doug said during our first full meeting on the subject. "How can your team learn to trust the validity of these employee productivity and effectiveness scores? Let's discuss overall metrics first, and then we can get into the specifics of staff performance. We've designed wireframe drawings of every dashboard page that we want Marie and Cassie to build, but essentially it breaks down into three categories, or 'Functional Areas' as we like to call them—patient access, revenue assurance, and patient financial services.

"Inside each functional area are over two hundred individual metrics that drive cash flow and help reduce net revenue leakage. We track things such as third-party rejections, unbilled claims, DRG anomalies, Medicaid conversion rates and third-party A/R greater than ninety days from discharge that haven't been resolved, multiple levels of productivity, and performance outcomes. Analytics are expensive, but here are a few of the wireframes to give you some examples."

With that, Cassie pulled up some mock-up screens on the large TV.

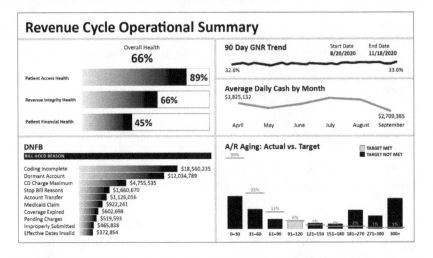

"This first screen is an overview of revenue cycle performance based on aggregate scores of the 200 metrics."

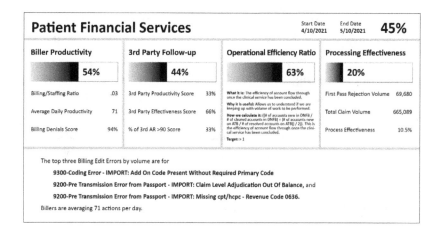

"This second one is down to the functional level, but you can see we've started to account for two of our measurements, both operational efficiency ratio and processing effectiveness ratio at the function level."

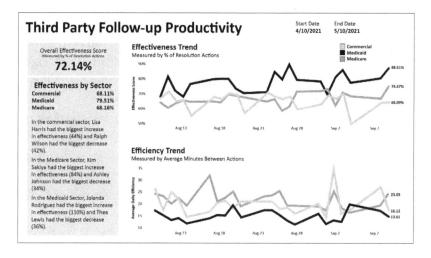

"And this mock-up shows how we'll start tracking staff productivity and effectiveness trends."

"These look great, Doug!" I was excited. "How soon do you think we can get all of this built out?"

"We can have some working prototypes for you in just a few weeks, but let me get you up to date on what the raw data is showing us. We've already discussed the improvements to staff productivity and effectiveness so far, but with our ability to track individual performance we've already begun performing some micro training. It's already paying dividends, as overall staff effectiveness has increased. As for productivity and the use of the Vispa system, there's a tracking feature that allows us to monitor how employees are being served accounts to work, and we've found that those using the 'Get Next Most Valuable' and the associated 'Peek' features, which give staff the next five most valuable accounts by the same payer they're currently talking to, has significantly improved productivity over those that are searching for accounts manually."

"Any lessons learned that you can share?"

"Well, it's also given us insight into modifying and creating action codes so they're appropriate for your environment, therefore maximizing the potential of your work prioritization and outcomes."

Integrated workflow findings, improved teaching techniques, and on-the-fly analytics. Now Doug had my full attention. "Perfect. Let's get Marie and Cassie rolling on this stuff right away. I'd like to see some working versions in two weeks. Marie, any other design concepts, or are we good to go?"

"I have two I'd like to share. In one of my visual analytic design courses, we learned that one of the best ways to track, monitor, and improve operational performance is to utilize two design techniques. One is consistently using the same visual component, like a graph, and the same colors. This enables rapid recognition by the human brain; so instead of determining what the graphic *represents*, the mind can jump right to what it's trying to *explain*.

"A second idea, with something as expansive as a full ecosystem revenue cycle monitoring solution, is the consideration of whether we should use a design technique that will allow any user to navigate through every department and figure out where underperformance issues originate from. It's a concept called 'guided discovery.' Basically, this means we'll have to put significant thought into the appropriate process-centered drill paths, so that as users continue to 'drill through' one visual to the next, it presents the next most logical visual to solve the root cause issue."

After carefully listening to Marie's recommendations, Doug asked, "So, will we be using these techniques for the McPherson Principle metrics as well?"

Marie calmly replied, "I can't see any reason why we wouldn't, but you're the industry experts. The metrics we want to use to measure performance can be calculated with a combination of back-end database tables in SQL and calculated fields in Tableau. I don't see any problem measuring and trending OER, PER, and EPR, along with all the other revenue cycle information."

After a few additional minor questions from the rest of the team, I requested that Marie and Cassie start working on the system and be prepared to give the team a weekly status report on Fridays. They agreed, and the meeting ended with excitement over the fact that we might be developing a revenue cycle analytic solution that has never existed.

▲▼▲

We continued down the path of fine-tuning the Vispa work prioritization solution, with "Action Taken" modifications to track employee activity, and improved data collection to track what actions a user took that had the highest payment outcomes, as well as incorporating more automation throughout the process.

As Marie and Cassie iterated the analytic solution each week, the management team was able to see each of their employees' performance on a firsthand basis and were able to identify and rectify problems that I never imagined we would have easy access to see. Negligible when considered from an individual staff level perspective, added together, these issues were causing serious positive disruption in the revenue cycle overall performance. The ability to aggregate seemingly disparate issues, identify systemic root cause issues, and have visibility into how small factors contributed to overall success, was amazing. With time, I was confident we would be able eliminate the majority of the issues, or greatly reduce them and drive even higher revenue cycle performance.

ICY DISCOVERY

August 15

AFTER TWO MONTHS of rapid implementation, daily firefighting, and constant staff feel-good sessions, it was time to take a step back and catch our proverbial breath. I decided to invite the team to the house for steaks and shrimp on the grill. Kyle was the first to arrive. Dave showed up next with his new girlfriend, Tiffany. Soon after was Marie, an interesting young lady in that she was comfortable with the crowd though new to the team. Kim showed up with her husband, Chris, a wild card always looking to ramp up the fun. Michelle came along soon after, a great worker but a quiet type who could go hours without saying a word. Doug and his team strolled in, completely comfortable. Finally, Shannon and her husband, Tim, arrived to round out the guest list.

Susan was the consummate Southern hostess, walking around helping everyone get a drink, asking if they needed anything, and passing around hors d'oeuvres. As I stood by the grill and surveyed my team, old members and new, I had to smile. Life is about surrounding yourself with those whom you trust and care about—it was a bonus that they were incredibly competent.

After dinner I sprang my surprise. "Hey, everyone. Can I have your attention? Doug and I were talking today and decided that this group needed a little friendly competition for the evening." I dramatically yanked a sheet in the backyard, revealing two giant blocks of ice. "The person who sits the longest gets a bottle of Irish whiskey," I announced, generating a few groans and catcalls from the group.

After several people declined, Doug looked around and said, "C'mon, Kyle, I know you'll take the bait."

"I'm game," he said, putting down his drink. "I'll do anything once. Twice just to make sure how I feel about it." The group laughed.

I noticed Shannon nudging her husband, who reluctantly stood up and walked to the ice cubes. He turned to Kyle and said, "Hey kid, get ready to lose."

I pulled out my phone and played "Another One Bites the Dust" on the patio's Bluetooth speakers. Everyone started to hoot and holler, heckling both guys as Doug got the event ready. "Gentlemen," he yelled with as much drama as he could muster, "on my command, take a seat and the timer will begin. One, two, three . . . SIT!" Both guys quickly plopped down on the ice and Doug started the clock.

Several minutes passed and I was sure one of them would give up soon, but I slowly began to realize that both were more stubborn than I'd originally imagined.

"I'm sitting here until the crown jewels are ice!" Kyle hollered.

"I'm winning that bottle!" Tim said in response.

They continued to banter back and forth for another fifteen minutes. Even though it had to be getting painful, they sat there and took it. As I watched, I had a surreal feeling that I'd seen this before, and then suddenly it hit me like I had just been struck in the stomach.

"Hot damn!" I exclaimed from the back of the group.

"What is it, boss?" Dave asked, a look of mild concern on his face.

"Tim, you're the winner," I said. "Kyle, I'll bring you another bottle on Monday. Let's gather around the fire and have a chat."

We moved to the recently lit fire pit, and I passed around my humidor of cigars for anyone who wanted one. Drinks in hand, I started to explain my epiphany. "It occurred to me while I was watching you guys that both of you were going to sit there as long as you needed, no matter how painful, until the other one gave up. I realized it's the same situation our staff is in when they interact with payer organizations. They work portals and get limited information, and when they do have to make a phone call, they will 'sit' on the phone as long as it takes to 'win' because that's what we've trained them to do. Because that's what we've always done."

"You got all of that from watching me sit on a block of ice?" Tim asked. "Wow, sometimes you hospital people think too hard."

This elicited quiet chuckles from the group, but clearly, I had struck a nerve with my team.

"My company's going through a digital transformation right now in our call center," Tim continued, "and we're using a 'smart dialing' system to allow us to remove wasted FTE costs from the work involved. Sounds like you could use some of the same technology."

"At the very least, we need to work on either changing the game or playing by different rules," Dave said. "It's time we dictated the way we interact with payers and not the other way around." He was displaying more emotion than usual.

I turned to our newest team member. "Marie, do we have enough granular data to measure how long each staff member is on with each insurance plan? If we do, then we can develop a strategy to reduce the wasted time."

"Yeah, I think we can do that. The time stamps from Vispa are down to the second. It should only take a day or two to implement."

"Make it happen. We could really be on to something here."

Eventually the party started to break up. On her way out, Kim stopped and turned to me. "Look, Bill," she said with a bit of a slur. "I know I'm a little drunk, but I just wanted to say that I've never been more proud of my work than in the last couple of months. Thank you for sticking with us and giving us this opportunity."

"Revenue cycle is a team sport, Kim. Thanks for all you do."
I gave her a hug, and she headed to the car. But as I shut the door,
I couldn't help but think that we weren't out of the woods yet.

OPTIMIZATION

September 8—Three Months until the Deadline

"Doug, I really hate to see you go. We've all gotten so used to having you around to help us work through our problems."

It had been Doug's last day on site, and I'd decided to drive him to the airport myself. We were at the American Airlines terminal, saying our goodbyes.

"Oh, come on Bill. You guys are doing great, and you can handle the optimization phase yourselves. And don't forget, Cassie and John will be around for another couple of months, and they've been through a few of these already. And of course, I'm just a phone call away. Let's stay in touch."

We shook hands. "Have a safe flight, my friend. I'm hoping we surprise you with results by the time you come back."

"I'm sure you will, Bill. I'm sure you will."

Back at the office I assembled the team in our war room. "Thanks for coming down on short notice, everyone," I said. "I just wanted to go over the final steps we need to complete in the coming weeks to fine-tune the Vispa system, as well as document some automation opportunities."

"I've asked Cassie to help with some of the automation documentation, if that's okay," Dave said.

Marie added, "And I've asked John to help with some of the complex Tableau development. Just FYI."

"Sounds good," I said. "To review, we need to work on using the 'Action Taken' tracking we put in place to understand what tasks staff members performed and categorize those so we can determine if there's a way to automate the process further. In addition, we need to start putting together trends related to staff performance, so we can fine tune the 'micro training' programs for each individual employee. Finally, we've been having a discussion around the need to focus on staff effectiveness reporting more than on productivity. Let me emphasize again that while productivity is important, staff effectiveness has a higher impact on revenue cycle results, so we really need to monitor EPR."

"Boss, I understand how to monitor EPR, but remind us why it commands so much focus?" Dave said.

"Let me explain it this way. If I'm doing follow-up work, for example, and I call an insurance company and leave a message to call me back, that would count as a '1' in the column for productivity, correct?"

"Yep, that's basically how it works."

"Let's say I do that fifty times today. What would be my daily productivity?"

"Uh, fifty?"

"Exactly. But what have I truly completed in that fictitious day of being on the phone that much?"

"Well, nothing really. But maybe the next day all those insurance companies will call back."

"Right, but let's stay focused for now just on that one day. If the total account balance for those fifty accounts was $100,000, and we assume for the sake of argument that all the balances are the same amount, how much money did my work contribute to the hospital?"

"Is this a trick question? It'd be $100,000. I mean, minus any eventual contractual allowances."

"No, Dave. It would be zero. I've done nothing that truly advances the account to payment. Now, assume instead of making phone calls, I already know the status of those fifty accounts, and I also know that they've all been denied for some billing issues. If I spend the day correcting twenty-five of the accounts and resubmitting to the insurance company, what is my productivity?"

"Twenty-five?"

"Correct. And how would that work compare to the same day of fifty phone messages?"

"You would only be half as productive."

"Correct again. But what would my contribution be to the organization based on the fact that I advanced twenty-five of the accounts?"

"I'm guessing $50,000?"

"Exactly. So even though I was 'slower' in theory, the work was more valuable to the organization. That's why effectiveness must be measured, *and* why it's more important than pure productivity. Now, the Holy Grail would be having both at a high level. The EPR would go through the roof in that situation, and then we're cooking with gas!"

▲▼▲

The next two weeks passed quickly, as the team and I continued to fine-tune the Vispa processes and configuration. As we approached three months post implementation, the hospital had already experienced dramatic improvements due to the automation and workflow systems. Also, the process effectiveness, operational effectiveness, and the other ratios were showing remarkable improvements. As I sat in Rebecca's office for my next leadership update, waiting for Terry to arrive, I was feeling confident.

"Sorry I'm a bit tardy," Terry said once he was there. "Had lunch with a few of the Board members and it took forever to get the check."

"No worries, Terry. Bill and I were just getting caught up on some day-in-the-life issues with one of our managed care payers."

"Nothing serious, I hope?"

"No, just some contract language clarification. Bill, why don't you walk us through your update?"

"Sure. I've brought some PowerPoint slides in case you wanted to share the info with the Board." I clicked the graphics from my laptop screen onto the big screen in Rebecca's office. "So, when we look at our key global metrics, we've improved both PER and OER by more than 20 percent since the last update. This is clearly an indicator of less human error from the pick-up of the RPA automation in patient access. Furthermore, we've improved employee effectiveness by approximately 20 percent and the productivity ratio by more than 30 percent, for an EPR increase of roughly 28 percent. All of this translates into a cash flow improvement of $7 million in just three months and a net revenue gain of 1.9 percent over that same time period. In addition, we've eliminated four of our open slots, and while it's not a direct cost savings, it's a cost avoidance of over $200,000 because we won't need to replace those individuals. Any questions?"

Rebecca looked concerned. "The numbers sound fine, but is your team doing okay? I know you all have been grinding hard."

"Actually, they're quite invigorated from being able to see how our decisions are impacting performance. The new metrics help a lot with that."

She turned to Terry. "Any questions before we let Bill go?"

"No, this all sounds great. The Board members I had lunch with are very happy with the results to date. Keep up the good work."

As I headed back to my office, I couldn't help but let a small smile creep across my face.

Wow. Terry and I may start getting along after all!

N L G

As WE REACHED the end of the fourth month of work, the team was now checking each system regularly and resolving the latent problems of every department, and the JHS staff was reacting positively to the network's minor changes. Kyle continued to identify opportunities for enhanced automation in patient access, while Michelle took hold of the RPA capabilities and identified opportunities to improve coding throughput by automating some of the background tasks related to the process. Dave also implemented some new action codes to track staff performance for a variety of activities that were missed in the initial configuration with the Vispa team.

Some of the supervisors were even reporting an upward surge in performance. This clearly showed the 1 percent methodology's effectiveness, and not for the first time I was glad we had included that in the supervisors' training.

After a couple of weeks, the team and I noticed that the analytics were working well and providing significantly greater insights than we had previously achieved with operations and staff performance.

Even better, the level of performance was so great that several department supervisors had let me know they had double-checked the numbers themselves just to make sure they were accurate. Upon reviewing the results, even I was surprised. I knew when we started that there were improvements to be made, or I wouldn't have put my job at risk, but the pace and magnitude of the improvements were nothing short of shocking.

I was explaining it all to Doug during one of our semi-regular Zoom meetings. "Have you ever seen anything like it?" I asked with pride.

"Oh, sure, I see this all the time."

I fake-frowned and said, "Well, I guess if I need my ego massaged, I'll have to talk to Susan."

He laughed. "Sorry. I mean I see improvement all the time, but your team has definitely set new expectations for my future clients. And speaking of improvements, I think we've finally reached enough granular data in your Tableau environment that we can really push the capabilities of Wordsmith, our Natural Language Generation platform. We should modify what we're reporting on to incorporate more root cause identification, as well as staff level insights."

"I'm game, Doug, but can you be a little more specific?"

"Of course. I'm thinking we can start identifying specific denials by specific payers, and which providers and services are the source. For example, for 'outpatient no authorization' denials, we can identify the procedure code and the provider in order to zero in on a fix such as education, process controls, etc."

"Can we really do that?"

"Absolutely. Marie and John have been putting some serious thought into the concept. Take a look at this mock-up." He clicked a button on his laptop, and I was now looking at his screen instead of his webcam.

"Wow. This is really insightful. How quickly can we get it into production?"

"I'd have to confirm with Marie and Cassie, but I would say within the next week. We'll need to do some data validation before we turn it loose."

Patient Access Process Rejection Analysis

Rejection Rate	Amount	Avg $ per Rejection	Volume
11.31%	**$36.80M**	**$5,885**	**6,252**

Rejections by Category

REMARK CATEGORY	AMOUNT	VOLUME
Authorization	$16,365,534	1,263
COB	$13,085,361	2,557
Eligibility	$7,340,083	2,484

Top 10 Rejections by CARC

CLAIM	AMOUNT
185	$12.75M
112	$7.05M
31	$4.22M
28	$3.15M
40	$1.64M
126	$1.15M
241	$1.03M
37	$0.68M
29	$0.64M
81	$0.58M

Rejections by Payer

	AMOUNT
Payer 1	$11.28M
Payer 2	$7.64M
Payer 3	$2.87M
Payer 4	$2.51M
Payer 5	$2.07M
Payer 6	$1.55M
Payer 7	$1.18M
Payer 8	$1.01M
Payer 9	$0.95M
Payer 10	$0.87M

The top Claim Adjustment Reason Codes (CARCs) among patient access rejections are **197** (precertification/authorization/notification absent) and **109** (Claim/service not covered by this payer/contractor). The number one payer for patient access rejections is **Rosemark Insurance**, with **11.28M** in Eligibility, Authorization, and COB processing errors annually. The top Remittance Advice Reason Code (RARC) on Rosemark Insurance remittances is **N185** (Do not resubmit this claim/service) with **$1.0M** in patient access rejections followed by N245 (Incomplete/invalid plan information for other insurance) with **$930K** in rejections. The top three DRGs rejected by Rosemark Insurance are **470, 314,** and **455.** The top three procedure codes rejected by Rosemark Insurance are **74177, 99283,** and **99284.**

Patient access rejections overall indicate that a significant process breakdown exists in the pre-registration process.

"Let's make it a priority. We could make even further progress if we have quick analytics at our fingertips. Doug, I really appreciate you pushing us in the right direction."

"That's why you hired us. I'll get the team working to finalize this right away."

"No worries. I promised Susan a seafood dinner tonight, so I'd better not be late."

During the drive home I thought about how far we had come in a few short months. I contemplated the use of NLG throughout our analytics and began to explore how we could tie in some additional visualizations around how staff get their work assignments and what actions they've taken. How can we generate best practice narratives, so that we can better understand how to train new employees in tactics that will drive the highest cash performance? When I realized that I'd made it to my neighborhood, I refocused on our coming seafood dinner and allowed myself to get excited about my coming blackened grouper with alfredo sauce. A perfect ending to a really good day.

FINE-TUNING

"**S**HANNON, WOULD YOU CALL THE TEAM and let them know I'd like to meet in an hour? Oh, and please have some coffee sent in."

"As you wish," she replied in her best *Princess Bride* Westley impersonation.

For most of the week I had been assessing both NLG and our newfound ability to analyze performance. Doug had been correct—some of the analytics we had available now were amazing. As I sat and pondered how to improve the insights even further, I thought about using the NLG feature to highlight staff performance trends. If we could do that easily and consistently, then we could study top performers and leverage their results to help the lower performers.

I got so caught up in it, in fact, I was ten minutes late to my own meeting, and had to deal with some good-natured ribbing about the team now being on "Matthews' Time." The excitement was clear on their faces, and I thought for the hundredth time about how far we had come.

"Okay, so I was thinking about adding into the NLG productivity pages some contextual updates, ones that would show the staff member who had the largest increase in employee performance ratio for each sector—Commercial, Medicare,

Medicaid—as well as the biggest decrease in EPR. Is that something we can do?"

"Yes," Marie replied, "we can do that easily with the daily data we're getting from Vispa. The granular level of the activity tracking lets us monitor what activities an employee performs during the day, so we can just categorize those actions into effective categories. Would you want that to be time bound, or allow the user to select the time period in question?"

"Marie, I love that you're always thinking one step ahead. Yeah, let's add in start- and end-date filters for the user. Nice touch. Dave and Kyle, I want you both to do a two-month EPR study for each staff member. Let's utilize the changes after Marie gets them added. We can leverage that information to evaluate our top performers and use the findings to help our lowest performers."

"You got it, boss."

"Now, my second idea is for Patient Access primarily, but centers around using NLG to provider deeper insight into the process effectiveness ratio. If we can improve our PER by reducing the number of initial payer rejections, that'll be a huge gain in cash flow and net revenue and allow our staff to focus on more important activities.

"Marie, I know we added in the NLG context for the top MS-DRGs during our last go around, and procedure codes for authorization rejections on the patient access pages, but is it possible on the outpatient side of things to add in the ordering physician? That way we could work proactively with the offices that are causing our largest volumes and try to get those reduced. If we can pinpoint the locations that are most commonly rejected, that will give us a leg up on figuring out the root cause."

"Whoa, great idea," Marie responded. "We have the physician NPI data in the related 837 claims data coming back from the payers, and we can link that to the 835 remittance data to tie the denial to the claim. If we use the account number as the key it should be fairly easy. What do you think about adding in the ability to filter by payer as well?"

"That would be awesome."

"Anything else while we're on a roll?"

"Yeah. Kyle, once we get the NLG set up to identify the physician, I want you to sample some of the accounts to confirm that they're correct. No need to upset any of our physicians by having faulty data. Once you're satisfied, then let's develop a plan to host some lunch-and-learn presentations with the respective practice managers."

"Sounds like a plan."

"On the coding pages, I'd like to link the coded accounts to the ones rejected for coding issues from the 835 data. If we can do that, we can hopefully pinpoint coding education opportunities for Michelle's staff. If we get the ones that cause errors identified, it should help with PER as well as the OER. I'm thinking if they're better at coding accounts correctly, they might also be faster. Michelle, is that something that will work?"

"Oh my goodness, yes. Sometimes without a full chart to bill audit, we don't have individual quality measures for the coding staff. This will help a ton in that department. Can I ask a favor, though? I'd like to have some additional insight into the average time to code an account, both by coder and by chart type. Similar to our collection efficiency data. If we could add that for coding, it'll tell me how my underperformers compared to their peers. That would really help zero in on improving the overall OER."

"Great, Marie, let's make that happen as well." Yup, we really were on a roll.

"All right, gang, I appreciate you all sitting through my thinking out loud. If anyone comes up with a cool piece of analysis, let's discuss it."

Kim looked up and said, "Hey boss, did we want to add in anything about the real-time performance that you and I discussed?"

"Oh gosh, I forgot to mention that one. Yes, I'd like to see if we can add in some real-time tracking throughout the day, maybe at fifteen-minute intervals, and then use NLG to determine when our staff are the most productive. This will allow Dave and his team to better understand if we can be flexible with work hours as well as comply with some of the 'work from home' requests. Marie, is that something we can do with the NLG?"

"I'll need to talk with the Vispa team, as they'll have to send us a file multiple times throughout the day, but I don't think it'll be a problem. Give me a few weeks on that one, but it should be doable."

I got lost in the rest of my day and headed home around 5:30. As I walked in the door, Susan and the kids were waiting for me with squeals and hugs. I looked at them with amusement and asked, "What's the occasion?"

"Babe," Susan said, "this is the fifth day in a row you've been home before six o'clock. We're celebrating a little return to normalcy."

"Return to normalcy! Return to normalcy!" the kids screamed, while running around in circles.

I guess a little fine-tuning at home is just as good as it is at work.

THE FINALE

October 29

WITH THE CLOCK TICKING toward the deadline for when I told Terry I would resign if not successful, I found myself pulling into the JHS parking lot, thinking that in only seven short months—not eight, but seven—we had achieved the improvements Terry had demanded—and more. I was on my way to a Board meeting to explain the results, and I couldn't have been happier. I had my presentation ready and my confidence was through the roof.

As I rode up to the executive suite, thoughts of the initial meeting popped into my head. Wow, how things had changed. Back then, I was so nervous I could barely think about standing up in front of the Board and giving a presentation. Now I couldn't wait to get in there and take a victory lap. Just like last time, I was in one of my best suits and was wearing Susan's favorite tie—the same lucky one I had worn last time so hopefully no one would notice. I had worked extra hard on the final presentation and had even had a customized presentation template made to provide some final "eye candy."

The room slowly filled, and then Terry kicked off the meeting. "There's a lot to cover today, and given Bill's performance over the past several months, some investments we need to discuss. Bill, if you'll get us started."

I stood up. "First, while I appreciate the compliment, I want to make clear that these are not 'my' results. The entire team worked hard to make this successful. That said, as everyone knows from the previous updates, we've made tremendous progress—even more since last month's meeting."

I clicked on my PowerPoint.

"As you can see by the table on the screen, in only seven months we have more than exceeded our goals, even including the additional investment costs. By significantly decreasing lack of authorization denials by our insurance companies, we've achieved more than a 2 percent net revenue improvement, or just under $40 million annualized. Staying on the denial front, we've reduced our medical necessity denials by more than 1 percent of annual net revenue, for roughly $22 million. Finally, we were able to control our untimely filing—and more importantly, our untimely follow-up—by more than 2 percent, and increase annual net revenue by an additional $44 million."

The Board murmured excitedly as I moved on to the next slide. "To date, we've totaled more than $106 million, after a goal of $80 million, and we think there will be even more, now that we have the right analytics to improve our transfer DRG billing for a few additional million."

Terry turned from the screen and looked at me. "Bill, these are amazing results, but will we be able to maintain them?"

"Yes, now that we have the Vispa solution and our newly designed revenue cycle analytics, we're confident that sustaining these results over time is very achievable, other than significant changes in contract performance or federal regulation modifications."

"Well, that's great news. Please continue."

"Right . . . okay, related to cash flow, we've made meaningful progress in leveraging the Vispa application on the coding front, and dropped our discharged, not final billed lag from a previous average of seven days to now roughly three days. This drove more than $20 million in one-time cash. Then by reducing our final billed, not sent volume in the claims scrubber from three days to an average of one day—which, by the way, is the industry standard—we were able to pick up another $11 million in cash flow. Finally, on the one-time cash flow front, we reduced our accounts receivable days by more than ten, three of which were liquidation, and the other seven were cleanup of old accounts. This amounted to another $16 million, for a total one-time cash flow gain of $47 million, crushing our assigned goal of $20 million."

"He's feeling a little cocky . . ." Jim Murphy said a little louder than he'd probably meant to.

I smiled. "Not cocky, Jim. Just really proud of the results the team was able to produce."

"Either way, impressive. How about the reduction in operating expense?" Jim recovered.

"Of course. That brings us to the final metric. By seeing a dramatic reduction in the need for FTEs in patient access, due to RPA and the additional gains by focusing on the employee performance ratio in patient financial services, we were able to reduce headcount by more than $1.1 million annually. While this is a bit below our 10 percent mandate, I'm hoping the higher-than-expected improvement in annual net revenue balances it out."

"I think we can let a few tenths of a point slide in this instance," Terry said, to the chuckles of the rest of the Board. "Before you go, can you give us your two cents on a few of the key factors in driving the improved performance?"

"Sure. While the technology helped both in terms of workflow enhancement and automation, I'm convinced our success was due to the continual focus on the McPherson Principle. By maintaining that focus on operational efficiency coupled with employee performance, we were able to constantly ask ourselves if we were making process modifications that were increasing the throughput of work. Combine that with the additional attention to process effectiveness, and you have the best of both worlds—extreme pickup in throughput with a high degree of quality improvements."

"One last question," Jim said. "How were you able to maintain your focus on those three measurements with all the changes going on?"

"Good question, Jim. Honestly, it was the 'power of 1 percent' concept. By monitoring the adjustments we made on a micro process level, we only tried to achieve a 1 percent improvement in any one activity. For example, if I wanted to improve the productivity of a staff member, I didn't try to get them to sixty-five accounts on day one. As long as the micro work was improving 1 percent a day, then everything was improving. It took some discipline, but once we started to get into a rhythm, it kind of became second nature. This is where the Tableau solution helped tremendously. We leveraged the analytics to work for us in that capacity, and then monitored the results, so we would know if something was wrong fairly quickly after implementing any specific change."

"Again, Bill, nice job. Very impressive work and results."

I smiled at Jim and nodded as I prepared to leave the room.

Terry stood up. "Bill, hold on just a second. After talking with Rebecca and then getting input from the Board, I wanted to let you know that we've created a new executive role, Chief Financial Sustainability Officer. This role will be tasked with analyzing our current and potential service offerings and finding ways to improve their financial performance. This will take someone who can think in new ways, see what others have seen but come up with different findings, and then drive those observations to improved outcomes. It's a big job, and one we believe vital to our future ability to take care of the communities we serve. We're all in agreement that after your remarkable performance with the revenue cycle transformation, you're the man for the job. I know I'm putting you on the spot, but what do you think? Keep in mind that it'll be a 50 percent increase in base pay, along with several other new perks."

I was floored, to say the least. Eight months ago, I was positive I was going to get fired; now I was being offered a C-level position. As I started to speak, I just hoped my tongue wasn't hanging out. "Uh, wow. Not sure what to say. This is a huge surprise and compliment. Can I have a little time to talk about it with my wife?"

"Of course. Take all the time you need."

"I'll get back to you in a few days. Thank you very much."

"No, thank you, Bill. Go enjoy the rest of the day with your team."

I nodded at Terry's last comment, still a bit in shock, and walked out of the boardroom as they moved on to other business. Once getting back, I called up Kim and asked her to step into my office.

"Of course you should take the job," she said. "You'd be great in that type of role."

"I have to be honest, it's intriguing. I've been doing revenue cycle work forever, and this would let me branch out. But I'd only take it if you'd be willing to take over my current position. I've put my heart into JHS, and I wouldn't want an outsider coming in and messing it all up."

"Oh my. Are you kidding me? I'd be honored, assuming Terry and Rebecca approve."

"I won't take the new role if they don't. This is too important to me. Oh, and I'd like to take Kyle with me to help with the analytics and planning. I'm going to need lots of support, and his energy is going to be a big help."

"Well, that'll be a temporary blow to that department, but during the transformation his assistant manager, Anita, really stepped up. She'd be a great fit to take over his current role."

"Okay, then it's settled. I think I'm going to take the rest of the day off and ponder some decisions. Think you can handle the place while I'm out?"

Kim just smirked, stood up, gave me a big hug, and then walked out the door.

I yelled at Shannon to let her know I'd be out for the rest of the day. Then I started to pack up my laptop, but stopped midway and decided not to take it home today. Time to celebrate with my one constant. Susan would be so surprised!

▲▼▲

"So that's the situation. With all the changes we just had to go through, the long hours and the time away from home, I wanted to get your thoughts before I made a decision." Susan and I were on the back porch, watching the sun go down, the kids horse-wrestling in the yard. I looked at her expectantly.

"My thoughts?" she replied, tearing up. "My thoughts are that you've been more excited about work over the past six months than I've ever seen you be. You love what you do, and you're so good at it, not to mention how much you care about JHS. Of course, you should take it."

"Babe, you really are the best." I picked up my beautiful wife and practically squeezed the stuffing out of her.

"How about we get my sister to come over to watch the kids, and we go out to the Italian restaurant you like so much. Maybe have a little too much wine, then come home and really celebrate." She had a twinkle in her eye that I never can deny.

"Deal. But let me call Terry first. If we're going to make a transition, let's go ahead and do it. Patience isn't really my thing." I pulled out my phone and dialed Terry's number.

"Terry, Bill here. I've talked to Susan and I'd be very happy to accept the new role, but I have a few conditions . . ."

I positively had to be the luckiest guy on the planet. Exciting new opportunity, three lovely children, and a wife I'd marry a thousand times over. Hanging up with Terry, I jogged back to the family, growled like a wolf, and jumped into the pile of my kids. The holidays would be great fun, after all.

Did I mention life is good?

ABOUT THE AUTHOR

MICHAEL DUKE'S thirty-year career has been spent asking the hard questions of how the healthcare industry can innovate administrative functions to remove as much human variability as possible, and codify work activities to remove wasted time and lost revenue for provider organizations. Michael's mission has been based on a firm belief that there must be a better way, and his career has been devoted to discovering it.

This effort led Duke, as he likes to be called, to the realization that the industry "standards" for monitoring staff and operational performance were outdated and prohibited new thought processes on how to monitor and improve performance.

Through the use of *The McPherson Principle*, Duke hopes to start the conversation on new metrics and develop an open dialogue about a better way forward, one that allows the industry to propel operational performance forward in a meaningful way.

Today, he is a committed leader with the Baker Tilly Healthcare consulting practice and works directly with clients to enhance their current position and enable their long-term success.

CPSIA information can be obtained
at www.ICGtesting.com
Printed in the USA
BVHW071444210621
610124BV00004B/990

9 781887 043991